I
KNOW
YOU

BOOKS BY ERIK THERME

Keep Her Close
Roam
Resthaven
Mortom

I KNOW YOU

ERIK THERME

bookouture

Published by Bookouture in 2019

An imprint of StoryFire Ltd.

Carmelite House
50 Victoria Embankment
London EC4Y 0DZ

www.bookouture.com

ISBN: 978-1-78681-924-6
eBook ISBN: 978-1-78681-923-9

For my buddy, Craig

PROLOGUE

Alissa Walker was a princess.

Bree suspected she was biased in this determination (as any proud, eighteen-year-old sister would be), but on Alissa's eighth birthday, Alissa could be anything she wanted—especially with a face as adorable as hers.

Freckled nose? Check.

Missing front teeth? Double check.

Blonde, curtained bangs that were constantly pushed away by tiny hands with pink fingernails?

How could anyone *not* love this kid to death?

"Tell me again how many times of *Sandy Spider* until my party starts?" Alissa asked.

Bree glanced up from the mixing bowl to check the clock. Alissa was in the early stages of learning to tell time, and for the most part, time was still measured against thirty-minute episodes of her favorite television show.

"It would be like watching four episodes," Bree told Alissa. "That's when the party will be."

"Awww," Alissa said, dropping her shoulders. She instantly perked up when their brother Tyler walked into the room carrying a brightly wrapped present with a flattened pink bow.

"That's mine!" Alissa squealed in delight, rocketing toward Tyler, who did what any respectable thirteen-year-old would do in the same situation: held the package over his head and out of Alissa's reach.

"Back off, squirt," Tyler said, grinning through a mouthful of shiny new braces—one of the many financial reasons they were hosting Alissa's birthday party home at their trailer, as opposed to somewhere that had pizza or games or annoying singing animals. "Your birthday isn't until eleven o'clock tonight, so technically you can't have it until then, and that's way past your bedtime."

"Technically" had become Tyler's go-to word these last few months, and Bree was two seconds away from adding it to the forbidden-words list, where it would join the ranks of "not fair" and "this is crap"—one of their mother's favorite utterances, which had been picked up by Alissa at an early age.

"Breeeeeeeeeeeeee," Alissa moaned. "Tyler's teasing me and won't give me my present."

Tyler lowered it just enough that Alissa could *almost* grab it. "It's not my fault you're not taller. Did you grow at all this year?"

"Just give it to her," Bree said, feeling the stirrings of a headache. It would be her fourth this week. "And don't whine, Alissa. You don't have to wait until eleven tonight, but you do have to wait until after dinner."

Alissa snatched the gift and carried it gingerly to the kitchen table, where she set it with the other two and began rearranging by size. Bree felt a pang of guilt that there were so few this year, but that guilt was replaced by annoyance when Tyler dropped onto the couch and stretched for the remote.

"No way," Bree said, carrying the dripping whisk to the sink over her cupped hand. "You promised you'd clean the bathroom if I made the cake and got the ice cream."

Tyler shook his head innocently. "That doesn't sound like something I'd agree to. And technically—"

"Bathroom," Bree said firmly. "Go."

A mischievous grin touched Tyler's lip, and Bree could only imagine what was coming next. Tyler was infamous for dragging out chores, and his current favorite was faking a sudden, inexplicable injury—anything from a sprained pinky toe to whiplash. Bree didn't have the time or patience for it today, and fortunately for her, Tyler seemed to sense this.

"Okay, girl," he said. Calling everyone "girl" was also a new thing, one Bree could tolerate but one their mother, Cassie, could not. "I'm just playin'."

Bree almost told him to stuff the gangsta talk, but he was off the couch and moving in the direction of the bathroom, so she would allow him that tiny rebellion. For now.

"But don't you ever get tired of it?" Tyler asked, stopping shy of the bathroom.

Bree's headache throbbed. "Tired of what?"

"Doing everything. The three of us are Mom's slave labor. How is that fair? We're kids."

"You really want to have this conversation again?" Bree asked, only half listening as she fed the cake pan into the oven. "You think Mom enjoys working two jobs? We're all a part of this family, and we each have our jobs to do—"

"Okay, okay," he said. "I've already heard this speech this month. Sorry for *breathing* and thinking this was a free country."

Tyler wisely slipped into the bathroom without another word. The kid had a mouth on him, but when push came to shove, he also knew better than to try to get out of chores. In the Walker household, everyone pulled their weight.

"And you, *girlie*," Bree told Alissa, wiping her hands on a towel, "have *still* not picked up the toys in the living room."

Alissa's head tilted. "But… it's my Special-Eight birthday. And when Julie Melick had her Special-Eight birthday, she didn't have to pick up any toys, and she got to eat her morning cereal in her bed, and she got a kitty and named it Bump because it bumped into everything." The injustice of all of this culminated in a tiny, troubled frown. "How come *we* don't ever get a kitty?"

"You want to know why?" Bree asked, but before giving Alissa a chance to answer she scooped her up around the waist. "Because it would eat all the toys you leave everywhere on the floor and poop them out all over the living room carpet!"

Alissa squealed in delight as Bree swung her around before depositing her onto the couch and tickling her until she squealed even louder.

"Really?" Tyler was standing at the edge of the hallway holding a toilet brush in a gloved hand. "I try to take a two-second break, but you guys get to lie there?"

"It's my birthday and we're *reacting*," Alissa said matter-of-factly.

"Interacting," Bree corrected with a wink. "Sisters always stick together."

Tyler shook his head. "Whatever. You two are redonkulous."

"Takes one to know one," Alissa said smartly, and stuck out her tongue. "So there."

Tyler raised the toilet brush in protest, but his face went slack as his eyes traveled past Bree.

"What?" Bree asked with a laugh. "Bump the cat got your tongue?"

When Tyler didn't answer or shift his gaze, Bree sat upright and saw their father, Jack, on the porch, looking through the screen door. In his hands was a scruffy, pink teddy bear that might have been salvaged from a dumpster. Bree scrambled to her feet and warily approached.

"What are you doing here?" Bree asked, immediately regretting her choice of words as her father's bloodshot eyes narrowed. Rule one was you never questioned Jack Walker, especially in "his" house. When he opened the screen door, it took all of Bree's resolve to stand her ground. Their father was two heads taller than she was, and despite his strict diet of alcohol and fried foods, he never took on fat, only muscle.

"We just didn't expect to see you so soon," Bree added quickly. "That's all I meant."

Three days ago, their mother had kicked him out for "loaning" their lot rent to a buddy to pay off gambling debts. Their father claimed he had no choice, because if the guy's wife found out, she would leave and divorce him, once and for all. Bree didn't know why their mother didn't do the same to their father. He was kicked out of the trailer every few months—sometimes peacefully, sometimes not so peacefully—but he was always eventually allowed back… when their mother was ready. As far as Bree knew, that hadn't happened.

"There's my princess," Jack said without a trace of a smile. His tone matched that of someone ordering off a restaurant menu. "The great, big, happy nine-year-old."

Bree didn't bother to correct him. It was a feat in itself their father even remembered today was Alissa's birthday. Alissa stayed at Tyler's side and said nothing.

"Come see me," Jack said, patting his outer thigh as if summoning a dog. He held out the bear in his other hand. "Get this thing and give me a hug."

When Alissa didn't move, Jack started forward, and Bree took a step sideways, positioning herself between them.

"You've been drinking," Bree said softly, "and you know how this works. Mom hasn't said it's time yet—"

"I'm not staying long. Phil's waiting outside in his van. I recently came into some cash, and we're going to hit the casino and win back your mother's precious lot rent money."

Bree wanted to reply with the obvious—it wasn't their mother's money; it was family money—but what was the point? Their father never cared for details. It didn't register that if the rent wasn't paid, they would all be evicted, or that whatever money he did have might be better served elsewhere. That wasn't how their father worked. For most people, even as little as five dollars would buy milk and bread for the week. For Jack Walker, it was five pulls of a slot machine and (in his mind) a chance to win big and change his life. The problem was, neither of those things ever happened and probably never would.

Alissa was now all but hiding behind Tyler, who was gripping the toilet brush so tightly that his knuckles had gone white. Jack's eyes slid from Bree to Alissa, then back to Bree.

"I don't need this shit," he muttered. He started for the door, stopped, and looked at the bear in his hand. "I don't need this shit either."

He chucked the bear at Alissa, who gave a surprised whimper when it struck the carpet by her feet. It was an asshole thing to do—a Jack Walker thing to do—but he was leaving, and in another few seconds, this would be just another crappy memory for the Walker record books.

"Who the hell do you think you are?" Tyler said savagely.

Jack stopped. Turned. Bree's stomach wrenched.

"What did you say to me?" their father asked, his voice danger-ously quiet.

"He didn't mean it," Bree said quickly, but it was too late. Tyler, like their father, had a temper that simmered just below the surface, and it didn't take much to set it off.

"What did you say?" Jack asked again, straightening to his full height.

Bree knew better than to try to talk their father down from something like this; she bee-lined for Alissa, lifted her with a grunt, and carried her into the back bedroom.

"Stay here," Bree said, setting her on the bed. "Don't come out."

Alissa caught Bree by the hand. "Don't go. I don't want Daddy to hurt you."

"He's not going to hurt me—"

"He will!" Alissa cried. Her voice was almost a sob as she clutched onto Bree. "He'll hurt you like he did before, but he can't if you stay here with me. That's all I want for my Special-Eight birthday. I don't want my presents, or even a cat, or even a cake!"

Alissa buried her face into Bree's chest.

"Listen to me," Bree said. "I need to—"

There was a sharp clap of sound, followed by an unintelligible cry from Tyler. Bree tried to rise from the bed, but Alissa held tight, refusing to loosen her grip. The screen door slammed.

"It's okay," Bree whispered to Alissa.

Alissa's breathing was labored and thick against Bree's neck. Just as Bree was about to try and pry herself free again, Tyler appeared in the doorway. The left side of his face was pulsing red, and there was a smear of blood across his cheek.

"Tyler," Bree choked. Alissa tried to turn her head to see, but Bree held it firmly. "Come here. Let me see."

Tyler drew back, his face caught between anger and terror. He didn't speak, but his eyes burned into Bree, blaming her, blaming their mother, blaming everyone but their father. He jerked away from the doorway and stormed down the hallway. When his bedroom door slammed, Alissa's fingers dug into Bree's skin hard enough to hurt. Her whole body was trembling.

"Shhh," Bree said, absently stroking Alissa's hair. "It's over. Everything's okay."

"Did Daddy hurt Tyler?" Alissa asked, her voice laced with tears.

"No," Bree lied. "Tyler's just upset. He's in his room now, taking a nap, so we need to be quiet and stop crying so we don't bother him."

Alissa sniffed. "I don't want Daddy to come back for my birthday party. I don't want him to yell or hurt us."

"He won't hurt us—"

"But he could. He could come back and hurt you or Tyler if he wanted to. He could even hurt *me*."

"Listen to me," Bree said, lifting Alissa's chin so their eyes met. "I will never let him hurt you. I will always keep you safe, no matter what I have to do."

Alissa blinked at Bree through her tears. "You promise? *Pretty* promise?"

"I promise."

Alissa threw her arms fiercely around Bree's neck and whispered, "I wish you were my mommy instead of my sister."

It wasn't the first time Alissa had said those words, and normally Bree would have told her not to think or say them, but today it was okay. Today Bree could be anything Alissa wanted her to be, because they were family, and the Walkers were survivors.

Nothing would ever come between her and Alissa.

Nothing.

CHAPTER ONE

Bree Walker was tired.

She was always grateful for overtime at the grocery, but standing for ten hours and dragging everything from milk jugs to cat litter across a scanner always took its toll on her back and knees, making her feel sixty-six instead of twenty-six. It also didn't help that she hadn't eaten since breakfast. Her lunch hour had been spent running fun errands such as getting an estimate for truck tires she couldn't afford, arguing with the bank teller over a late fee, and returning an armful of stupid romance novels to the library (for her mother) that were already two weeks overdue. All Bree wanted to do now was eat, drown herself under a hot shower, and relax for a few hours before her mother arrived home from her late shift at the restaurant.

"It could always be worse," Bree mused, smiling at the dilapidated AUKES TRAILER PARK sign as she drove through the entrance. It was her mother's favorite saying, second only to "work smarter, not harder"—a slogan more repeated in their family than practiced. But it was the truth. Things could always be worse. Instead of still living at home with her mother and now sixteen-year-old sister Alissa, Bree could be homeless. Instead of a truck with no air conditioning, the truck could have no heat. Instead of contributing her paycheck toward the family fund of groceries and utilities (and everything else it took to sustain their existence), Bree might be forced to choose between spending her money on new clothing, travel, or something else that might be fun and break up the monotony of the day, week, or month. Who needed that headache? Not her. She had learned long ago that good things did not always come to those who waited—another of her mother's sayings—and you played the cards you were dealt, good or…

"Bad," she sighed as the truck rolled to a stop in front of their trailer. Alissa's backpack was sitting on the front step. It had been two days (this time) since Alissa had "run away" from home, and their mother had been nagging Bree to fetch her. Not that Alissa's whereabouts were a secret. Alissa always went to stay with her best friend Liz, who only lived a few streets over in the newer addition to the trailer park. The "fancy" side, as their mother called it. The side where the majority of the trailers were double-wide, the pipes didn't freeze in the winter, and the residents didn't spray-paint their dead lawns green to give the illusion of grass.

Bree killed the engine, feeling a simultaneous sting of relief and dread. On one hand, she didn't have to go and drag Alissa home now, but on the other hand, she wasn't in the mood to deal with her—not with the prospect of food and relaxation in her sights. She knew sitting in her truck was only delaying the inevitable, but at least it gave her a moment of peace. Once inside, Alissa would unload her typical emotional speech about how horrible life at home was, and how no one in this family understood how hard it was to be young. And from there, Alissa would deftly segue into the real reason she had left in the first place: Bree shouldn't have yelled at her, and just because their mother worked all the time and was never home, that didn't give Bree the right to *act* like her mother.

It was an old, repetitive argument, and one that Bree was beyond tired of having. Bree got it: Alissa was sixteen and knew everything about everything. It was a teenager's prerogative to question and defy everything. But Bree never talked back like Alissa did, or sulked inside her room for days over petty arguments. A few months ago, Alissa had invited a boy (Austin?

Anthony?) over after school, and then freaked out when Bree wouldn't let them shut the door when they went into Alissa's room. That had earned Bree the silent treatment for almost an entire week. Bree had no regrets. Alissa was naïve when it came to boys and what they *really* wanted, while Bree knew too well. She could count on one hand how many boyfriends she'd had in high school, and she'd given them all the boot when they got too handsy. It wasn't that she didn't like boys; she just found them mostly stupid and juvenile. Someday the universe would challenge her with someone worthwhile, but until that time, she wasn't too worried about it.

Mr. Nortman, their neighbor, was parked on his porch in a lawn chair as always, dressed in his Hawaiian shirt, cargo shorts, and a cloth-brimmed sun hat, looking like a tourist in a faraway land. He was facing the opposite direction and holding a pair of binoculars at the trailers behind them. Their mother always called him a dirty old man, but he had never made lewd comments toward Bree—something that couldn't be said about some of the other older men in the trailer park. Mr. Nortman was also hard of hearing, and he hadn't glanced over once, even though Bree was halfway up the driveway.

"Now, Mr. Nortman," Bree said, raising her voice, "I know you're not looking into Ms. Murray's trailer."

Without missing a beat, Mr. Nortman raised the binoculars into the tree line above, and then turned his head. "Oh, it's you, Bree. Beautiful weather we're having, and the sparrows are out in droves." He held out the binoculars. "Care for a look?"

"I think I'm good, thanks."

"I'm happy to hear that. And your mother, Cassie? Is she good?"

"She's good."

"Excellent. And Alissa?"

Mr. Nortman had limited conversational skills and they usually stuck to the same script of questions and answers.

"Sixteen and strong-willed," Bree answered with a resigned smile.

"I understand completely. And Tyler? Is Tyler well these days?"

Bree nodded without comment. It had been almost a month since she had seen or heard from her younger brother, but it wasn't uncommon for Tyler to disappear for long stretches with no contact. Tyler's restless nature kept him on the move, but never in a productive way. He avoided work at all costs, spent most of his time hanging out with shady friends, and his sleeping arrangements were dictated by whatever female he was shacking up with that week. He still *technically* lived at their trailer (or a handful of boxes with his things did, anyway), and he did occasionally show up to eat or crash on the couch, but those times were few and far between. Which was probably for the best, as there was usually something missing when he left. Loose change that had been left out on the counter. A package of toilet paper or a jug of milk. Never anything major that couldn't easily be replaced, but it frustrated Bree to no end. Being a part of a family meant *contributing* to the family. Tyler was a good kid overall; he just needed to get his shit together and grow up.

Mr. Nortman was nodding thoughtfully, leaving Bree to wonder, again, how much he saw, and how many times over the years those binoculars had been turned onto their trailer, focused on their windows. Now he was going to comment on their father, saying (again) how much of a shame it was the way things had worked out, but he must have seen something on Bree's face, or spotted the circles under her eyes, because he only lifted his binoculars and shifted in his chair.

"Don't let me keep you," he told her. "Run along and have a good evening."

"You do the same, Mr. Nortman."

Bree took the wooden steps, picked up the backpack with a heavy sigh, and was surprised to find the door locked. Alissa wasn't the paranoid type, and it was rare she even *closed* the front door when she was home, even while showering. No matter how many times Bree scolded Alissa about it, the response was the same: "I'm sixteen, not six, and I can take care of myself." Bree longed for Alissa to be six again. Or even seven or eight or nine. Hell, she'd even take ten or eleven. Bree still missed doing fun, sisterly things like shopping, riding bikes, and taking trips to the library. Back before those wonderful hormones took over and changed everything.

"I'm home," Bree called out. She didn't expect a response but was still disappointed when she didn't get one. She dropped the backpack and peered down the hallway. Alissa's door was shut, like always, but unlike the front door, it wouldn't be locked because it didn't have one. Alissa had been lobbying to have a lock installed going on three years now, but their mother had stood firm, saying none of the bedroom doors had locks, and there was no reason to spend money to keep people out. That wasn't how family worked. Bree was fine with that. She had nothing to hide. She had no secrets.

"Did you eat?" Bree asked loudly, peeking inside the Crockpot. Their mother often got creative with leftovers and was fond of "mixing-and-matching" foods by dumping everything into chicken broth. Tonight's feast appeared to be ham and kale and nasty-looking mushrooms, which might have been okay if it hadn't smelled like dirty laundry. A frozen pizza was definitely in her future.

She picked up the mail from the table, unsure if it was from today or yesterday, and began thumbing through it. Mixed within the bills was a postcard from a car dealership promising zero interest for six months. Bree slipped it into the recycling bin, hoping Alissa hadn't seen it. On top of everything else, the last thing Bree needed tonight was to restart Alissa's complaining about not having a car to drive. There was already enough complaining about other things. It wasn't uncommon for Alissa to randomly bring up something they had argued about days ago, as if the conversation had merely been on pause, and—without warning to Bree—they had inexplicably circled back to it. Important things like the location of Alissa's phone charger (usually lost within the blankets of Alissa's bed); why there was no food in the cupboards (which *really* meant Alissa's favorite foods like popsicles and candy); or who moved Alissa's five pairs of shoes (that had been left in the middle of the living room for the umpteenth time).

Bree looked again at the hallway. Still no peep from Alissa. It was Wednesday, which meant their mother would be at the restaurant until well past midnight if they got a rush of last-minute customers, which they usually did. It was just after seven now. Bree knew she was stalling and trying to put off the inevitable, but she couldn't pussyfoot around the trailer all night. She could wait for Alissa to come out, or she could go in there and get it over with.

As if on cue, her phone dinged. That would be Alissa, texting because it was too much effort to open her bedroom door or yell through the wall. And Bree doubted it was an apology. But it wasn't from Alissa; it was from the number (555) 123-4567.

I can help you

Bree frowned. It wasn't uncommon for her to receive messages meant for the girl who had this phone number before her (she had learned long ago that Peggy was clearly very popular with the boys), but those texts usually came in late at night. Bree messaged "wrong number" and started to set down her phone. Immediately, the message bubble with three dots appeared. The person on the other end was typing.

You're Bree Walker

It wasn't a question. Bree warily lifted her phone, ice trickling down her spine.

Who is this?

The response was immediate:

A friend

"A friend," Bree said under her breath.

She wasn't in the mood for this. One of the grocery store supervisors had probably given her number to a co-worker who needed a shift covered.

"Help with what?" she asked aloud as she typed. She set down her phone and started toward the bathroom when the phone dinged again.

Save your sister

CHAPTER TWO

Bree stared at her phone without blinking. Her feet sent her in the direction of Alissa's room before her head had fully turned. She knocked on the door once—a quick rap—before opening it without waiting for an answer. The futon where Alissa slept was a pool of blankets, sheets, and pillows, but no Alissa. Bree checked the closet, knowing there was no way Alissa could be inside—not with the number of shirts mashed together on plastic hangers—before checking the window, which was locked from the inside. She went back into the hallway and did a quick sweep of the bathroom and the other bedrooms—all empty—before returning to Alissa's room and looking again, as if Alissa might have magically materialized in the few seconds Bree had been gone.

"Alissa?"

She wasn't there. Bree returned to the living room to make sure she hadn't hallucinated seeing (and picking up and carrying) Alissa's backpack, and then dialed Alissa's cell phone. It rang four times and went to voicemail. Bree hung up without leaving a message—Alissa never listened to them—and instead texted:

Where are you?

The message sent. Bree watched the screen, waiting for a reply as the seconds bled past. Satellite reception in the trailer park was spotty, and paying for monthly internet and Wi-Fi wasn't a "good use of financial resources," as her mother would say. Any second now, Alissa was going to text back. Her backpack was there, which meant Alissa had been there. Alissa had stopped by the house, dumped off her belongings, and gone out with some friends, acting like nothing had happened. That was so Alissa. The text was from one of Alissa's friends, messing around with her phone, sending messages like "I can help save your sister" because Alissa was probably flirting with a boy at the mall, or something dumb like that. Bree could almost visualize Alissa's friend typing as Alissa, laughing so hard she was crying, was trying to get the phone back out of their hands.

There was still nothing. Bree backtracked to the main screen and contemplated the (555) 123-4567 number, which obviously wasn't real. The text, of course, was real, but she knew there were websites out there that let people hide their numbers by using fake caller ID or spoof websites. That alone was enough to set off her creepy meter, but the fact that the text mentioned her sister (and Alissa hadn't been seen in two days) made it all worse. Bree started to respond with, "Who is this?" then changed her mind and texted:

You know my sister?

She sent the message, but instead of waiting for a reply she tried Alissa's phone again. As soon as voicemail picked up, she ended the call and dialed again. Voicemail. She did this four more times, hoping Alissa would answer out of annoyance, but knowing it wouldn't make a difference. Alissa's ringer was always set to vibrate—something that endlessly annoyed Bree—as it allowed Alissa to use the excuse, "I never heard it ring," which was crap, because the girl always had the phone in her pocket or in her hand.

"You leave me no choice," Bree said, searching out Liz in her contacts and dialing.

Liz picked up on the first ring. "Hello?"

"Hey, Liz, it's Bree. Alissa isn't answering her phone for me, so will you tell her it's time to come home? And by that, I mean now, not two hours from now."

There was a pause. "Alissa isn't here."

"Of course she is. She always goes to your place when we get into a fight."

"Well, yeah… but she really isn't here. My dad and I went to South Dakota last weekend and just got back this morning."

Bree's mouth opened and closed. It wasn't that she thought Liz was lying, but Alissa not being there had caught her completely off guard.

"When was the last time you spoke to Alissa?" Bree asked.

There was another hesitation. "We had some weirdness between us before I left, kind of an argument, and I haven't talked to her since then. I mean, I sent some texts, but she never texted back." Another hesitation. "You really don't know where she's at?"

"No. Can you try calling or texting her and let me know if you get ahold of her?"

"Yeah. I'll do it as soon as we hang up."

"Thank you."

Bree's heart rate gained speed as she ended the call. Frustration and fear mixed inside her stomach, creating a pit of nausea. Alissa hadn't stayed with Liz, but that still didn't mean she was in trouble. Alissa had other friends, and if she and Liz were fighting, it would make sense for her to stay with one of them. Now the problem was finding *which* friend. Liz's was the only number she had. Their mother might have an idea, but it was unlikely, and as both Bree and Alissa knew, you only called Mom at work in dire emergencies, as in "someone's head had accidentally been chopped off" or "the trailer was flooding *and* on fire."

"Damnit," Bree muttered.

This was just like Alissa. She was the textbook example of the kid who always had to be the center of attention, good or bad. On the last day of school, Alissa had spray-painted the word CHEATER on the windshield of her gym teacher's car. Apparently, there had been a rumor going around that Mr. Cobb had been playing his own version of dodgeball (or *balls*, Bree imagined) with his new female assistant between classes, and Alissa had taken it upon herself to right that wrong. Alissa admitted later that it was only based on a rumor, and *maybe* she hadn't thought her actions through. It had been a miracle their mother hadn't strangled her—especially since she had to leave work in the middle of her shift—and she might have if Bree hadn't been at home to calm everyone down. Because that was Bree's job: to keep everyone calm. To play devil's advocate, mediate and mitigate, and try to keep the household running smoothly.

There was still no reply from 555 or Alissa. Alissa was supposed to have the "read notification" feature activated, but she never did, and it had caused so many arguments—"What are you, the government? You don't need to know exactly when I read my messages"—that their mother had given up and let it be.

Bree's eyes went to Alissa's backpack as she mentally paged through scenarios. Had Alissa even come inside the trailer? Had she just chucked it onto the porch and driven off with someone? Walked off? What direction? Was she with anyone else? The backpack hadn't been there when Bree had left for work—she was certain of that much—and their mother would have said something if she had noticed it on her way out. Whenever it had been dropped off, it couldn't have been that long ago. In fact...

Bree pushed out the door, jogged down the steps, and crossed the yard. Mr. Nortman was still in his chair, swiveled now in the other direction to violate someone else's privacy across the street. He lowered the binoculars and raised his eyebrows at Bree.

"Squirrels," he said briskly. "Two of them, fighting in that tree—"

"Have you been sitting here all afternoon?" she asked.

"The complete and utter numbness in the lower half of my body tells me yes."

"Did you see Alissa earlier? Maybe in the last few hours?"

He shook his head. "The last time I saw Alissa was Monday evening, I believe. She was coming out of the trailer"—he leaned forward and pointed past her—"trying to get away from you."

Bree remembered it well. As did most of the neighbors with open windows that night, Bree imagined. The argument had been a doozy: both of them shouting at each other over whose turn it was to unload the dishwasher. The fight should have never escalated past dirty looks and snarky comments, but Alissa had been more emotional than normal that night (girl problems, was all she would say), and Bree had been exhausted and irritated and unable to hold her tongue. When Alissa had stormed into her bedroom, thrown clothes into her backpack, and run out the door, Bree hadn't tried to stop her. She had actually been relieved... until their mother came home later that night, scolding Bree for letting Alissa leave. From there, it didn't take long for the guilt to seep in, because their mother (as always) was right: Bree should have never let Alissa go. It didn't matter that Alissa had been insufferable since school had let out for the summer; Bree was the adult. She was the glue. And if Bree couldn't keep it together, they weren't going to make it.

"Alissa's backpack was on the porch," Bree said to Mr. Nortman. "The one she took with her when she left that night."

"I see," he answered, but it was clear he didn't. His attention was already waning, tracking a woman who was jogging past.

"Her backpack is here," Bree said, struggling to keep her tone neutral, "but Alissa isn't. You said you've been sitting here all afternoon, which means you would have seen her bring it home. Did you?"

Mr. Nortman blinked in her direction. "Did I what?"

"*See* Alissa? Have you seen her today?"

"Not that I recall." His eyebrows lifted. "But I have seen a strange car in the neighborhood these last few days. Once of those fancy new SUVs. Sometimes it's parked across the street, and sometimes it's down the street, and sometimes it's even parked in the front of the entrance to our park."

The last thing Bree was interested in was new neighbors or what they drove. "I—"

"But I did see someone that wasn't Alissa in your yard earlier," he added. "I couldn't tell you the exact time, but it would have been in the afternoon, shortly after your mother left for work, but before Chris and Karen from down the street arrived home."

Bree stared at him, waiting for more. "Who was it? Who did you see?"

"I can't be one hundred percent," he said, motioning to his driveway with the binoculars, "seeing as how my station wagon partially blocks my view of your trailer, but I'm seventy-five percent sure it was Simon Foster."

She knew the name. Everyone in the park did. The Fosters lived in the corner trailer at the end of the street, and Simon was a twelve-year-old delinquent known for terrorizing small animals, destroying flower beds and gardens, and generally causing trouble at every possible opportunity. Simon's father was roughly the circumference of a refrigerator, regularly in and out of prison, and proud of it. It was only a matter of time before Simon and his delinquent brother, Lane, followed in their father's footsteps.

"Did you see Simon with a backpack?" Bree asked.

"He might have had something in his hands." Mr. Nortman gave an apologetic shrug. "I wasn't paying that close attention. Ms. Hamer was walking her dog, and I was too busy wondering if she had fries to go with her shake." He laughed at his own joke, and then sobered when Bree didn't join in. "I'm sorry. I don't mean to make light of your situation. I hope Alissa returns home soon. I'm sure she will."

"Thanks," Bree said automatically, already heading down the street. Her pulse increased to match her footsteps. The rational part of her knew Alissa was going to turn up any second now, just like she always did… but it was her irrational side, like always, that spoke louder. That side conjured up images of human trafficking, murder, and every other horrific, unimaginable thing lurking in the world. Because this time was different. In the past, Alissa had always stayed with Liz and returned Bree's texts, even if it was with snarky comments like, "I'm never coming home," or, "You're ruining my life."

The Fosters' trailer was just ahead. It was easily one of the oldest in the park and had odd-shaped windows, no curtains or blinds, and metal siding the color and texture of rust. Alissa always joked it looked like something out of a horror movie, and Bree agreed: the only thing missing was a snarling Rottweiler on the end of a chain, and aluminum wind chimes made from beer cans. Simon was nowhere in sight, but his fifteen-year-old brother, Lane, was cranking a wrench on a dirt bike that looked as if it had been dragged straight out of a junkyard. His eyes crawled over Bree as she approached.

"S'up, Breezy?" Lane asked with a catlike grin. He was shirtless and probably weighed all of ninety pounds soaking wet. Unlike Mr. Nortman, Lane never hesitated to make googly eyes and crude comments in her direction.

"Where's Simon?" Bree asked.

"I dunno. Inside?" Lane was wiping his hands on a greasy rag and flexing his tiny biceps. "What did he do this time? I can fetch him."

"Get him."

Lane swept the hair from his eyes as he raised his head. "Simon! Get out here!"

"Why?" came a muffled voice from inside.

"Cuz I said so!" Lane gave a rickety laugh. "Kids, huh?"

Bree crossed her arms and said nothing. She couldn't see any movement inside the trailer, but there was a prolonged clatter—as if something had been knocked over by accident or in frustration—followed by a high-pitched string of mild profanity.

"You look nice today," Lane said.

"Really? You think I look nice? Is it because of the dark bags under my eyes, or is it that my hair smells and feels like damp hay because I haven't showered since yesterday morning? Do tell."

"Damn... you sure don't know how to take a compliment. I don't know why you're always so rude to me. I'm only trying to be friendly. Remember last week when I came around and asked your ma if she wanted someone to mow your yard?"

"And I'm sure that had nothing to do with me washing my truck in a bikini top."

Lane looked offended. "I was offering my services—"

"I don't want your compliments, and we don't need your 'services.' If you want me to treat you like a human being, then stop talking like you're a gangster pimp, and never again call me Breezy. Got it?"

"Yeah," he scoffed. "I got it."

The trailer door thumped open. Simon crossed the lawn wearing a pair of dry, blue swim trunks, possibly because it was the only clean thing he had to wear. Rumor had it that their mother had skipped out on them a few weeks ago, and their father hadn't been sober long enough yet to notice. Under other circumstances, she might have felt sympathy for the kid. But not today. Not if he knew something about Alissa.

"What do you want?" Simon asked. His lips barely moved as he spoke, and his eyes, too small for his face, had a rodent look. "I was on level twenty-eight of *Star Crashers*."

"Where did you get it?" Bree asked.

"Get what?"

"Don't play dumb. Alissa's backpack. Where did it come from? Why did you have it?"

Simon's cheeks went crimson. His mouth stayed open, but nothing came out.

"I know it was you," Bree said. "Mr. Nortman saw you walk up to our trailer and put it on our porch."

Simon looked at Lane, then back to Bree. There was no way this kid was this stupid. The park was too small to get away with much of anything. Someone was always watching. Someone always saw everything.

"This is serious," Bree said, taking a step toward Simon. "Alissa's been gone two days now, and we don't know where she is."

Lane's face scrunched. "Alissa ran away again? Was it because of all that yelling the other night?"

"Stay out of this," Bree said.

Simon eyed his brother as he stood a little taller, clearly trying to impress. "Why should I tell you anything? All you ever do is yell at me to stay out of your yard and away from your windows and your truck."

"I'll handle this," Lane told Bree. "I can make him spill his guts. He does whatever I tell him to do."

"No, I don't," Simon said.

Bree's patience continued to slip. "I don't have time for games—"

"No games," Lane said, "but it'll cost you. I'll make him tell you… in exchange for a squeeze."

"What?" Bree snapped.

Lane grinned and playfully cupped his left pec. "You know, a quick squeeze. What do you say?"

"You know what?" Bree said without hesitation. "That sounds like a fair trade. One squeeze it is."

Lane's mouth dropped. Before he could speak, Bree latched onto Lane's left nipple with her thumb and forefinger, and twisted as hard as she could. The noise that left Lane's lips was something between a banshee wail and a dying calf. He dropped backward into the grass like a bag of rocks, both hands clamped over his pec as a sound rose and died in his throat.

"I don't give a *shit* that you're an idiot," Bree said, standing over him, "or that you're only fifteen, or that your dad might be inside, watching this right now. I only give a shit about my sister, and if your brother doesn't start talking right now, I'm going to reach down and give something *else* of yours a squeeze—"

"Okay," Lane rasped, tears in his eyes. "Tell her, Simon!"

Simon took two steps back, eyes wide with shock. "Someone gave me the backpack to put on your porch."

"What do you mean *someone*? Someone *who*?"

"I don't know!" The words began pouring out of him in out-of-breath bursts. "It was some guy. I was riding my bike near the front entrance, and he walked up carrying it and asked if I knew where Alissa Walker lived and said he'd give me ten bucks to return her backpack. All I had to do was put it on her porch."

"Did you know him?" Bree asked.

"No," Simon squeaked. "He said not to ask any questions if I wanted to get my money. So I didn't. I wasn't going to pass up ten bucks!"

Simon shot a fretful glance toward Lane, who was still on the ground, breathing heavily, his face contorted and constricted. Bree's head was buzzing with so many questions she could barely think straight.

"You never saw him before?" Bree asked. "Are you sure? What did he look like?"

"He smelled and his clothes were dirty. He looked like one of those homeless guys who sit on the corners and asks for money. He watched me from the other side of the street and he wouldn't give me my money until he saw me put the backpack on the porch. I don't know any more!"

Bree took out her phone as she started back toward her trailer, fighting to hold onto her anger so that the fear lying just underneath wouldn't overtake her. She dialed Alissa's cell again, disregarding Mr. Nortman as he leaned forward in his chair to watch Bree enter the trailer. When Alissa's phone went to voicemail, Bree ended the call, started to dial her mother, then stopped cold when her eyes fell on Alissa's backpack. She hadn't thought to look inside, and now, after everything that had happened, she found herself not wanting to… but knowing she had to. Because the backpack hadn't stayed with Alissa; it had come back to the trailer. Been delivered. The question was *why*?

Bree bent down and worked the zipper with unsteady fingers. Nothing exploded. The inside wasn't drenched with blood. What was inside was clothing. Alissa's clothing. Bree lifted out a blue flannel shirt that had been hers before being liberated to Alissa's wardrobe last year. Beneath that were jean shorts, a knot of rolled socks, and fancy underwear that Bree was positive their mother hadn't purchased and certainly wouldn't have approved of. There was also Alissa's birthday present from their mother: an instant mini camera that spit out playing-card-sized photographs that developed when exposed to air, just like those old Polaroid cameras.

Bree dug deeper, removing Alissa's wallet, makeup bag, phone charger… until, at the very bottom, she saw a plain, white envelope. It was creased down the middle, as if it had once been folded in half. Nothing was written on the outside, but Bree knew it was for her to find. She knew it with every ounce of her being.

She slowly reached inside and took it out. It was unsealed. She lifted the flap. Inside was a photograph of Alissa sitting on a concrete floor surrounded by concrete walls with both knees drawn into her chest.

Below that, written in marker:

IF YOU TELL ANYONE SHE DIES

CHAPTER THREE

The photograph slipped from Bree's fingers and landed on the carpet. Bree stared at it in horror. Alissa was wearing a blue tank top with red stripes and jeans—the same outfit she'd been wearing two nights ago—and her hair was tucked behind her ears, revealing a pale, terrified face.

"Bree?"

It was Liz, Alissa's best friend, who Bree had just talked to on the phone, standing there, face white, mouth open, gaping back in utter shock. But not at Bree—at the photograph on the floor.

"Is this real?" Liz asked, picking up the photograph. It trembled in her hand. Bree gave no answer, because they both knew it was. It wasn't trick photography; it wasn't a tasteless joke. Someone had taken this picture. Someone who now had Alissa, somewhere, for some reason.

"Where did you get this?" Lines of fear crossed Liz's face. "Who gave you this?"

"Save your sister," Bree said… and everything fell into place with a sickening punch.

Bree fumbled out her phone and scanned through the previous texts from the 555 number. Bree's last text was still on the screen, unanswered:

You know my sister?

Bree dialed the number and pressed the phone to her ear. It began to ring. And ring. Her stomach tightened, waiting for someone to answer or even for a voicemail, but there was only endless ringing. Bree took the photograph from Liz and checked the backside for anything she might have missed. There was nothing else.

IF YOU TELL ANYONE SHE DIES

This was real. Alissa had been taken. Abducted. It wasn't a movie or a story in a book or something she was watching on the ten o'clock news. Tears stung Bree's eyes and it took all her concentration to type:

I will do whatever you want. Tell me what you want.

Hysteria threatened to overtake her again, and she forced it back down, commanding herself to keep it together. That was how she was going to get through this—by keeping a clear head. Alissa always accused Bree of being indifferent and devoid of emotion, but what she never understood was Bree didn't allow herself to be controlled by her emotions, because the rare times she did—like the dishwasher incident—things spiraled out of control. Staying calm, rational, and analytical was the answer. She needed to focus on one thing at a time and ignore the bigger picture. Alissa had been taken for a reason, and whoever took her was in contact. They weren't going to answer the phone when Bree called. Bree could send as many texts as she wanted, but it wasn't going to make a difference. She had to admit that. Until the abductor was ready, there was nothing Bree could do. Unless…

Bree selected the Locate My Phone app. Bree knew their mother often used it to make certain Alissa really was where she said she was. It was also handy as hell for finding lost phones, as Alissa had somehow lost hers a few weeks back while out for a walk, and the app had led them straight to it.

She entered Alissa's e-mail and the password of WALKERFAM-ILY—the same one they all used so it was easy to remember—and a compass appeared on the screen and began to spin. Bree held her breath as she waited for Alissa's phone location to appear on the map, but after a few seconds Bree's hopes were dashed when only two green dots appeared on her screen: Bree's phone, along with her mother's. But what did that mean? The abductor had deactivated the GPS on Alissa's phone? Blocked the signal? Was that a thing?

Liz was dialing her phone. "I'm calling the police."

"No," Bree said, jerking the phone from her hand. "You can't."

"What do you mean *no*?" Liz's voice was shrill. "Alissa has been gone for two days, and I come over here and find a picture of Alissa in a... is it a jail? We need to tell someone—"

"There's no one to tell. And we can't call the police. The person who took Alissa said not to, or they'd kill her."

"And you just believe that?" Liz shook her head. "You don't know anything about this person. The police know how to get things done. They can trace the phone and catch him and find Alissa. He won't know we did it. I see it all the time on television."

"This isn't television," Bree said sharply. "Things go wrong. The police make mistakes, and people can get hurt and die. Do you really think the police care about what happens inside this trailer park? Do you know how many times over the years my mother or I had to call them on my father, only to have them show up thirty minutes later, acting bored and indifferent like we were wasting their time?"

Bree's phone dinged.

Find Tyler.

"What?" Bree croaked.

Bree sent a return text in a rush, barely striking the correct keys as autocorrect fought to keep up:

What does my brother have to do with this?

Liz inched forward, sneaking a peek at the screen. Bree paid her no notice as she waited for a reply. Her hands twitched as the message bubble appeared, hovering on the screen endlessly, until finally:

Bring me Tyler and Alissa goes free.

All the strength left Bree's legs. She reread the message. Then read it again. And again. Tyler had caused this. Of course it had something to do with Tyler. Everything bad that happened to this family was because of Tyler or their father.

Bree's phone dinged again:

You have until midnight.

She swallowed against her closed throat. She started to type, "What happens at midnight?" but there was no reason to. It was as explanatory as the picture and words. There was only doing what she was told, following instructions. And these instructions didn't get any simpler. Tyler had done this, and Tyler was the only one who could fix this. He was somewhere. She had more than four hours to find him. She had time. She could do this. She could do this, because it was what had to be done, and it was as simple as that. As long as she kept her shit together, everyone would get through this. Overthinking was as bad as losing control of her emotions.

Bree dialed Tyler's number, unsurprised when she received a disconnected tone. Tyler only used prepaid cell phones (or burner phones, as they were often called in the movies) that could be purchased at any retail store and didn't require cash or contracts. Because of this, his number always changed, and during those times there was never a way to get ahold of him until he randomly resurfaced at the trailer. Right now for Bree, her brother was no more than a ghost.

"Go home," Bree told Liz. "Go home and don't say anything about this to anyone."

Liz looked like she had just been slapped. "You expect me to go home and do nothing? Alissa's my best friend—"

"And she's my sister. You don't think I'm freaking out right now and on the verge of losing my mind? You think I don't want to run screaming to the police?"

"Then call the police—"

"We *can't*." Bree's neck flushed with anger. "I already told you that. You saw what was written on the picture. What they said they would do. We don't know what this person is capable of. We don't even know if it's just one person. All we know is they took Alissa, and if we call the police, they'll—" Bree stopped herself short. She couldn't bring herself to say it. "Hurt her," Bree finished. "And I'm not risking that, especially since we know what they want. They want Tyler."

Liz's chin was trembling. "And what happens then? What happens to Tyler?"

Bree started to answer, then realized she didn't want to. If she yanked on that thread, it wouldn't stop and the horrible possibilities would consume her. Once she found Tyler, they would cross that bridge. It wasn't like she was just going to hand him over.

"Go home," Bree said again. "If you hear anything or think of anything that could help, you call me. Me. No one else. Do you understand?"

Liz dropped her eyes but gave a hesitant nod. Bree hated that Liz had been drawn into this, but what was done was done, and hopefully Liz wouldn't do anything stupid. She gave Liz a final glance before exiting the trailer.

"Where are you going?" Liz called after her.

Bree said, "To find my brother."

CHAPTER FOUR

Tyler sat slouched in the passenger seat beside Bree with his arms crossed. On the bench seat between them was Tyler's birth certificate and a copy of his failed learner's permit test. It was the third time since Tyler had turned fourteen that Bree had taken him, and the third time they had driven home in dead silence. And now the fun would continue into the night, when Tyler would moan and mope about how all his friends had their learner's permit and he didn't. Bree braced herself as she wheeled into the driveway and killed the engine. Tyler remained in his seat, staring out the window, grinding his teeth.

"Don't say it," he said, even though Bree hadn't uttered a word. There was no reason to. They both knew the routine by heart.

Bree: "Did you study for the test?"

Tyler: "It's the same questions every time."

Bree: "Then what's the problem?"

Tyler: "They purposefully make the questions tricky to confuse you."

Bree wasn't sure if she believed that, but it had been almost five years since she had gotten her permit, so she was willing to give Tyler the benefit of the doubt. Not that it would change anything. Tyler was only interested in approaching things on his terms, and until he adjusted that mindset, things like learner's permits were going to remain out of his reach.

"Listen," Bree said, "what if—"

Tyler opened the door, climbed out, and slammed it with more force than was necessary.

Bree exited the truck and made her way up the driveway. Tyler was already inside the trailer, undoubtedly taking out his frustration on Alissa, who fortunately knew to ignore Tyler when he went into one of his rants. But Tyler wasn't ranting; he was standing stiffly inside the front door.

"Tyler?" Bree asked.

She stepped inside and saw their father sitting at the kitchen table with a beer. It was just past three o'clock, which was two hours before he should have been home from work. There were only two reasons for their father to come home early: he'd lost another job, or he'd been called away for some reason.

"Where are Mom and Alissa?" Bree asked uneasily.

Their father took a long drink, wiped his mouth, and set down the can. "They went to the store. Sit down."

Bree started for the chair.

"Not you. The boy."

Tyler hesitated but only for the briefest second. He took the chair across from their father without a word, crossed his arms, uncrossed them, then dropped his hands into his lap.

Their father finished off the can, set it aside, and cracked another. "Patty Abrams called me at work today," their father said. "Do you know who that is?"

Tyler's eyes flicked to Bree's. "That's our aunt... right?"

"More or less," their father answered. "My half-sister from out east. She's only visited once, when you were just a runt. Alissa wasn't born yet. She married some insurance or car salesman or something like that. I never met him. They have a son, Seth. He's close to your age."

Their father took another drink. Bree remembered the visit well. Patty had been an enormous, pear-shaped woman with a mountain of curly black hair and a dry, hacking cough. The only time the woman stopped smoking was when she ate or used the bathroom. Bree couldn't remember the exact reason for the visit (in the area for a wedding, maybe), but Bree had been relocated to the couch for those two days. Her room had stank of cigarette smoke for weeks afterward.

"Seth is dead," their father said. "He killed himself yesterday. Put a gun into his mouth and blew out the back of his throat."

"Jesus," Bree whispered, putting a hand to her mouth.

Their father's hand tightened around the can hard enough to crinkle it. He was looking at Tyler with an intensity that frightened her.

"I was running the forklift when the shift supervisor pulled me off the floor. Told me I had a phone call in the office. I thought maybe it was your mother. Bad time for a call. We had two trucks waiting to be unloaded, and we were already behind schedule. I tried to tell the supervisor that, but he said the woman insisted on talking to me. Said it was an emergency." His face soured. "Seth was already dead. How is wanting to tell me that an emergency?"

Bree bit her tongue as their father drank again. She didn't want to hear anymore, because whatever was coming next wouldn't be empathy or compassion; she knew that much.

"Patty's husband left her a few months ago," their father said. "Apparently, I'm the only family she's in touch with, so she called me. She wanted money. Can you believe that? My half-sister who I never see wanted money, from me, to help pay for her dead son's funeral." His lips curled. "I was so pissed over the call that the shift supervisor sent me home, saying I wasn't in a fit state of mind to finish the day."

"What did you tell her?" Tyler asked.

It was the wrong question to ask. Their father's gaze sharpened as he leaned forward in the chair. "What part of this is confusing? The part where she's my half-sister and barely family? The part where she only calls when wants a place to stay or money? Or is it the part where her stupid-ass fifteen-year-old son kills himself for no good reason. And by 'no good reason' I mean I'm sure he had reasons—I didn't ask—but only a coward does something like that. A real man faces his responsibilities. He doesn't run from them. He doesn't take the easy way out. What the hell is wrong with you?"

"Nothing," Tyler said huskily. *"I just—"*

"You kids today know nothing of real problems or pain. Your feelings get hurt, and you want someone to talk to about it, or you want to get medicine to fix everything. But you know what? Life isn't always easy. It's not supposed to be. Being challenged is what builds character. And being a man means working a job, supporting your family, and standing up for yourself. Do you hear me?"

Tyler's face had lost a shade of color. *"Yes."*

"You better." He eyeballed Tyler as he drained the can and added it to the other empties. Instead of reaching for another, he began rubbing his hands together. Slowly. Roughly. *"Your mother was sixteen when she got pregnant with Bree. We didn't plan it. Neither of us was prepared. And there were times… many times… that I wanted to do something drastic. Get in my car and leave town. Drink myself to death. Anything to escape. And do you know where you'd be now if I had done any of those things?"*

He paused, as if wanting an answer, but spoke again before Tyler had a chance.

"You'd be nothing," he said. *"Never born. Non-existent, just like your half-cousin Seth is now. You only exist because I owned up to my responsibilities. And someday, when you start sticking your pecker into girls, you better be smart about it or you'll find yourself married and with kids, and you'll be me, and that would just be too goddamn bad, wouldn't it? But at the end of the day I have my self-respect, because I learned to roll with the punches and suffer the consequences. So don't do anything stupid like knock up your girlfriend or kill yourself. How hard is that? Think you can manage that?"*

Their father cracked another beer and shook his head in disgust. *"Now get out of here,"* he said. *"Both of you."*

A motorcycle blew past in front of Bree's parked truck, startling her awake from her thoughts. The dashboard clock said she'd been waiting almost fifteen minutes now, and she returned her attention to the apartment building across the street—or, more specifically, the clump of teenaged boys on the sidewalk tossing furtive glances over their shoulders as they passed something amongst themselves. Bree couldn't discern if it was a dirty magazine, liquor, drugs, or something worse, but until they left and weren't blocking the building's main entrance, she thought it to be in everyone's best interest to wait. That's what she told herself, anyway. But she also knew she was stalling. This was the last place she wanted to be, and she had told herself she would never step foot inside under any circumstance. But circumstances had changed.

Her cell phone rang, and a lump rose in her throat when she saw it was her mother. There was no way Bree could talk to her. Not now. If she did, she would break down and spill everything, and that wouldn't be good for anyone. Her mother would never understand how delicate the situation was. It wasn't her mother's style to be tactful or discreet. Her answer was to strike back with a jackhammer. Hit them harder than they hit you. Use a knife, when all that was needed was a letter opener.

The phone went quiet, and Bree prayed there would be no voicemail. Their mother had zero tolerance for unreturned phone messages. She waited a few moments, checked to make sure she hadn't missed a return text from the 555 number, and pocketed her phone. The teenagers were finally slinking off: two groups of two in opposite directions, exchanging middle fingers, laughs, and colorful profanities. One of them glanced in Bree's direction as they passed and offered up a smirk. Then they were gone, and Bree was out of excuses. It was time.

She exited the truck and crossed the street, gathering her nerve. Never mind that all she wanted to do was curl into a ball, close her eyes, and pretend none of this was happening. Having those thoughts didn't change the cold, hard facts. Emotions were the enemy, and emotions could be controlled. They could be pushed aside. Pushed through. It was okay to feel afraid, as long as it didn't stop you from doing what needed to be done. It was one of the ways that Bree was like her mother, and it had served her well over the years.

The other teens were around the corner now, out of sight, but there was a lanky guy leaning against the far wall that Bree hadn't noticed before. It was hard to discern his age with his hoodie thrown over his head, but his posture suggested he was somewhere in the neighborhood of her age. An unlit cigarette clung to his lower lip, and she could feel his eyes on her... inside her.

"Hiya," he rasped, breathing the word more than speaking it.

She gave him a sharp nod as she yanked open the door. From the corner of her eye, she saw him roll off the wall, and as soon as she was inside the building, she knew she had made a mistake. The hallway was cramped, dimly lit, and completely deserted. She headed straight for the set of metal mailboxes on the wall by the staircase and willed herself not to turn when the door opened again behind her. The guy had followed her inside. She slowed just enough to glance at the names on the mailbox—WALKER, APT 7—before continuing quickly down the hallway, scanning the apartment numbers as she passed. The last door was 6. She needed the second floor, which meant taking the staircase, which thankfully wasn't enclosed. The guy was closer now—she was sure of it—and she took the staircase at a jog, wrestling her key ring from her pocket and positioning the ignition key so it stuck out from between her knuckles. By the time she reached the second floor, her heart was going a hundred beats a minute and she cursed when she saw the apartments were 11 and 12. Apartment 7 was on the far end.

She hurried down the hallway, sneaking glances over her shoulder, almost tripping on the frayed carpet. The door to apartment 7 was no more than an arm's reach away. Before she could knock, the guy materialized from the staircase around the corner, sending her backward in a series of startled, blundering steps.

"Stay away from me!" she spat, raising her keyed fist.

"What the hell, lady?" The guy lowered his hoodie and innocently raised his hands. His face was even worse in the light: pockmarked cheeks, yellow teeth, and an oily head of long, black hair. "What did I do?"

"You're following me."

"I ain't *following* you. I went out for a smoke and checked my mail." He swung his hand toward the opposite door. "I live in number 8."

"You expect me to believe that?"

"Lady, I don't give a damn what you believe," he said, moving sideways toward the other apartment, hands still raised. "I'm just trying to get back into my apartment without getting keyed in the face. What the hell is wrong with you?"

Bree's face flushed. She didn't apologize or take her eyes off him, but she did lower her fist as he dug inside his pocket, presumably for his apartment key.

"I don't blame you," he said, shooting a sullen glance in Bree's direction. "This is a shit neighborhood, and I wouldn't trust no one either. But people need to understand that sometimes decent people have to live in shit buildings and neighborhoods, because it's all their family can afford. That don't make them bad people. It just makes them poor."

He freed his key ring with a grunt, also dislodging a mess of quarters from his pocket that went rolling in every direction across the hallway carpet.

"And there goes my damn laundry machine money," he said with a groan, dropping to one knee and collecting the coins. He nodded toward the floor behind her as he continued to scoop. "Can you at least grab me those quarters by the wall?"

Bree turned without thinking, seeing only a discarded gum wrapper. "I don't—"

It was all she got out before he lunged at her legs, knocking her to the floor. A burst of air exploded from her lungs as she hit the carpet sideways, arms flailing, trying to kick him off, but it was too late. He crawled on top of her, one hand clutching her hair, the other pressing a short knife to her throat.

"Stay quiet," he hissed. His face was inches from hers, close enough to taste the alcohol on his breath. Greasy strands of his hair brushed her cheeks as his head turned side to side, checking the hallway. "Lucky for me, no one gives a damn about anyone else, especially in this neighborhood. But if you yell, I will cut you. I don't want to, but I will. You think I like doing this? I don't. But I do what I have to do to survive, so I need your cash and your credit cards."

Bree pulled a long, gasping breath. "I don't have any."

"Do you not *get* this? I'm holding a knife to your throat. One swipe and you're bleeding out on this carpet, dead. Do you want to die?"

"No," Bree whispered, pinching back tears, "but I don't have any money on me."

"Where's your purse?" he asked, glancing around the floor, as if it might be hiding in plain sight. "You had one when you came inside."

"I didn't. I don't carry a purse."

The guy's lips drew back in a grimace. "Then where do you keep your driver's license?"

"In my back pocket."

"Exactly. Along with your cash and your credit cards." He abruptly released his grip on her hair. "I'm going to check your pockets, and I'd advise you not to wriggle, otherwise my hand holding the knife might slip. We clear on that?"

His hand burrowed into her front pocket as the blade pressed deeper against her neck. She wanted to scream, lash out, but she only stared into his bloodshot eyes as her fear turned into revulsion then anger as his hand explored the pocket, probing each side, lingering near her crotch. When he removed his hand from her pocket and dragged his fingers lightly across her exposed stomach toward her other pocket, she seized his wrist in her hand. The look of surprise on his face was beyond comical, and it was clear he was too stunned to react.

"Get off me," she said through clenched teeth.

The blade bit into her neck, sending a sizzle through her skin. He had drawn blood. She was sure of it.

"You really don't get this," he told her, but his voice was shaky, all at once unsure. He tried to free his wrist, but she refused to let go, tightening her grip even as he applied more pressure to her throat with the knife. "I will cut your head off—"

"For what?" she seethed. "My driver's license? I already told you I have no money. So get off me, because I swear to God, if you *touch* me again, I'm taking you with me."

The guy's Adam's apple swelled to the size of a golf ball as he swallowed. This was going to end badly—not because she had pushed him too far, but because he didn't know what to do next, and he was too stupid (or spiteful) to simply climb off and walk away. He was in over his head, and they both knew it. He had messed with the wrong girl on the wrong night.

"If you do what I tell you," he finally said, "I might let you live."

Bree sucked in a breath. "And if you don't get off me in the next five seconds, you're going to get your head kicked in."

"Yeah? And how do you plan to kick my head in when you're pinned on the ground?"

"Because I'm not doing the kicking," Bree said with a stiff, upward nod. "*He* is."

The guy managed a half turn before a mouthful of boot sent him sprawling sideways with a howl of pain. Bree kicked herself free and scrambled backward as the guy tried to right himself while cupping a hand over his bloody mouth.

The guy said, "I'm gonna kill—"

His last words died in his throat as he eyed the monster of a man hovering protectively over Bree, and it took him all of one second to realize this wasn't a fight he wanted to pursue. The guy struggled to his feet, spat a bloody wad of mucus onto the floor, and retreated down the hallway without another word.

"Shit," Bree whispered.

The man reached down, took Bree by the crook of her arm, and effortlessly lifted her onto her feet. The pungent smell of his aftershave sent a wave of emotion flooding through her, and as soon as she steadied herself, she jerked away, using the wall for support.

"You sure know how to make an entrance," he told her.

Bree said, "We need to talk… Dad."

CHAPTER FIVE

Bree shifted uncomfortably in the armchair as she held a wet paper towel against her neck. The inside of her father's apartment was nothing like she expected. Her father had never been one to burden himself with personal belongings, and other than his clothing (which mainly consisted of tank tops and jeans) he had nothing tangible to account for his forty-odd years of life. But there were framed pictures on the walls, an ottoman for the armchair, a couch, coffee table, and even a rug. All of these things were dated and looked as if they had been acquired from second-hand stores or garage sales, but it was a far cry from what Bree had imagined his apartment to be: a single room with a recliner that doubled as his bed; an ancient television with a clothes hanger antenna; and maybe a few books sitting in a corner. Bree did note there was a pair of women's sandals in the corner by the door, but she wasn't about to ask who they belonged to. She was there for one reason and one reason alone.

"I need your help," Bree said as her father returned from the kitchen. He had been insistent on making them tea—something she would have never imagined her father drinking in a million years. "It's about Alissa."

Her father said nothing as he handed Bree her tea, set his mug on the coffee table, and settled onto the floral couch across from her, which groaned under his six-foot, two-hundred and-fifty-pound frame. It had been six months since they had last spoken, but her father looked the same: cropped gray hair, thick beard, and penetrating blue eyes—just like Tyler's. The only noticeable difference was the small scar on his forehead, just above his left eyebrow. That scar was also six months old, and also from the last time they had spoken. She knew this because she had a companion scar on her hand from where the coffee pot had shattered after swinging it into her father's head.

Her father still hadn't spoken. He lifted the mug from the coffee table as he studied her. He had never been a man of many words.

"Did you hear me?" Bree asked. "I said I—"

Her father raised a finger and Bree instantly silenced herself, more from years of conditioning than anything else. The finger was IN CHARGE—something she, Tyler, and Alissa had learned at a very early age. Finger goes up; mouth stays shut.

"First things first," he said. Her father had a low, bass voice that demanded attention, and all at once she was a child again, feeling as if she had done something wrong. She hated herself for feeling this way, and she hated her father for making her feel this way. "How is your neck?"

Bree lowered the paper towel. There was blood on it, but only a little. She touched the cut with her fingers and found it dry. "It's nothing."

"Good. Whoever that was, he doesn't live in that apartment, and I don't think he'll be back to this building again. I see no reason to call the cops and overcomplicate things. Do you agree?"

"Yes," Bree answered mechanically, because this was how it worked with her father. If she wanted an audience with him, it meant playing by his rules and showing him respect. "Thank you for helping me."

Her father leaned forward and began wringing his hands. His unblinking stare continued, making it difficult to read his expression, but something about him was different. Something had changed. He almost looked... *uncomfortable* was the word that came to mind. It was a side of her father Bree rarely saw.

Being uncomfortable was an emotion, and outside of anger, her father didn't do emotion. Emotion was a sign of weakness. It was the one trait they both shared, just not to the same degree. Bree chose to control emotion. Her father was simply incapable of it.

"I'm sorry I had to come here," Bree said. "If I had another choice—"

"Your hair is longer than it was before."

Bree found herself at a momentary loss. "Excuse me?"

"Your hair," he said, motioning at her with two fingers. "It's long. It makes you look more like your mother. Do you know that?"

"I didn't come here for a social visit," she said briefly. "I need your help."

"And I haven't seen you in half a year, and I imagine that once you get what you want from me, I might never see you again. So how about we at least try and play the role of father and daughter, even if it's only for five minutes. I think you owe me that much."

Heat rose inside her belly, and it took every ounce of her self-control to keep her mouth closed. The last thing she was interested in was who owed what to whom. She was a fool to think her father was going to willingly help. He would take five minutes, or fifteen minutes, or however many minutes he wanted, because the word "unconditional" didn't exist in her father's vocabulary. Bree wouldn't get what she wanted until her father was good and ready.

"Any boyfriend in your life I should know about?"

"No," she said, "my fifty-plus hours at the grocery store doesn't leave much time for romance, and most of my free time is spent cleaning, doing laundry, or trying to study for the single community college class that we can barely afford and that I'm barely passing."

Now he would lose his temper. Now she'd see the Jack Walker she knew and loathed. But he only nodded, seemingly more to himself than her, and motioned toward her untouched tea.

"You should drink that. Lots of herbs and antioxidants and other stuff to keep you healthy. Sue drinks about three cups a day."

Sue. The name hung in the air like bait. Bree wasn't going to give him the satisfaction of asking. She didn't care if Sue was a neighbor, his parole officer, or a girlfriend. She suspected the latter. It explained the sandals. Bree didn't bother to remind him that he was still married to her mother. Not that her mother wanted him back. Divorce lawyers were expensive, and once Jack had moved out, they both knew it was over. There was no reason to waste money on a piece of paper. Neither of them had anything of real value.

"Sue lives here," her father said. "With me. She's a lovely woman. You'd like her."

"Why?"

He set down his tea. "What do you mean?"

"Is it because she's pretty? Smart? Is she a hard worker? Do we share the same taste in music?"

His face darkened at Bree's tone. "I only meant that she's a nice woman. I'm making pleasantries. We met at Alcoholics Anonymous. She changed my life."

And there it was. The "new and improved" Jack Walker now made sense. None of this was about trying to reconnect; it was only a pathetic attempt to prove something. He had overcome his demons; straightened out his life; and now, in his mind, all could be forgiven. But it didn't work that way. Not by a long shot.

"Our family is in trouble," Bree said, struggling to keep her voice even, "and instead of helping me, you're sitting there, making 'pleasantries' about things that don't matter. You think I care that you quit drinking? Or that you're shacking up with a new woman who you think I'd *like*?"

"Watch yourself," her father said sharply. "When you're in my home you will show me respect—"

"Because you deserve respect? Is that what you think?" Bree rose to her feet as her anger boiled over in a rush of words. "Do you think anything you say or do can erase the years of hell you put our family through? Is that what they tell you at AA? Everything can be forgiven? It can't. You don't get to take back the things you did. So let's stop this bullshit and let me talk so I can get out of here and we can all get on with our lives."

Her father was also on his feet now, the tendons in his neck bulging like ropes. The last time Bree had dared speak to him this way, she had ended up with a fractured rib.

"Hello?" said a timid voice.

They both turned. The pudgy woman in the open doorway had red hair as large and majestic as a lion's mane, and her facial foundation was laid so thick it was impossible to discern a single wrinkle or line. In her hands was a cardboard box overflowing with cross-stitch supplies and patterns.

"Is everything okay?" the woman asked, maintaining a fragile smile as she glanced back and forth between them. "Am I interrupting something?"

Her father inhaled deeply through his nostrils. "Everything's fine, baby. We have a special visitor."

"How exciting," the woman said brightly. She set the box on the kitchen table, brushed off her hands, and strode across the room with her left arm extended. "It's very nice to meet you. I'm Sue Spangler. Who might you be?"

"Bree Walker," Bree said as they shook.

Sue's penciled eyebrows lifted. "You're... your name is *Bree*? But isn't... aren't you...?" A squeal of delight escaped her mouth as she looked at Jack. "It's your daughter, honey. She's come to visit!"

"Yes," he said quietly.

Sue looked as if she wanted to burst. Literally. Her hands jumped from her bosom to her cheeks to her chin, before finally coming to rest on Bree's arm, but only long enough for a light, affectionate squeeze.

"I just can't believe it," Sue said breathlessly. "I mean, I had always hoped I'd get to meet Jack's children, but Jack always said—"

She stopped short, stole a cautious glance at Jack, and bit her lip. Bree felt a shiver of disgust toward her father, who had clearly set boundaries that Sue had almost crossed.

"I should make some food," Sue said carefully, as if weighing each word. "Should I? No. I should probably leave you alone. Do you want me to leave you alone? I should go. Should I stay?"

"Bree says she has something important to tell me," Jack said. "Maybe it's best if you give us a minute."

"Of course," Sue said, nodding fervently. "The last thing I want to do is interrupt. You sit down and have your tea and don't mind me. I'll be quiet as a mouse." She was already backing away, gathering her box from the kitchen. "I'll be in the bedroom, Jack. Bree, it was *so* nice meeting you. I hope you do come back and see us again real soon."

Bree managed a strained smile as the woman skittered down the hallway, wobbling side to side on pink heels. The bedroom door shut. Her father was still standing, but his chest had deflated, and his eyes were fastened on the floor.

"Your five minutes are up," Bree said tonelessly. Her pain and anger had subsided as quickly as it had surfaced. She had no time for it. No place to put them. She only stared at her father, hollow-eyed, waiting for whatever came next.

"What do you need from me?" he asked. "Money?"

In her father's world, most problems were solved with money or violence. Her father didn't believe in diplomacy. He had no consideration for others. Even if Bree took the time to explain everything from the backpack to the phone call, the simple fact was that the end result involved Alissa. He wouldn't care that she was taken. He wouldn't accept that she was in danger. He would just assume it was a cry for attention or one of those "female games" that all women liked to play. And even if he did accept the truth, in his mind, it would somehow be Alissa's fault. Something she deserved. Karma. The only way Bree was getting what she wanted was by leaving Alissa completely out of the equation.

"I need to find Tyler," Bree said.

Her father lifted his head. He didn't speak, but his eyes narrowed, searching her face, trying to gauge her intentions. Tyler was her father's only soft spot. The notion of "Daddy's Little Girl" had no place in the Walker family. Jack Walker was one hundred percent ground-beef of a man, and damned if his son wasn't going to be as well. Growing up, if Bree stood up for herself or talked back, she got "what she deserved" for being disrespectful. If Tyler stood his ground, he also got a beating, but at the same time, it also earned him respect. Their father was fond of bragging to his friends: *That boy can take a hit.* Jack Walker was no pussy, and neither was his son, and watch out to anyone who thought otherwise.

"Is Tyler in trouble?" her father asked.

"Have you seen him?" Bree asked.

The room lapsed into silence, save for the humming of the refrigerator. Bree told herself to answer his question. To not get caught up in this bullshit war of wills. But she couldn't. Because it wasn't about being stubborn—another trait, she begrudgingly realized years ago, she shared with this man; it was about proving to him she was worthy of his information. Of course her father had seen Tyler. Of course he knew where Tyler was. They had a relationship that Bree had given up trying to understand long ago. The question was how far their father would go to try and protect Tyler, which begged the bigger question: how much did her father know, and was her father somehow involved with whatever Tyler had gotten himself into? She didn't think so, but she was about to find out, one way or another.

"Well?" she asked, her tone demanding an explanation. It took all her resolve to not blink, swallow, or move.

After a stalled silence, her father lowered his chin and ran a hand across his mouth. Now he was going to come at her. Finish what the guy in the hallway had started. She dared him to try. Instead, he gingerly raised his index finger—*wait*—and made his way down the hallway toward the closed bedroom door. Bree watched as he knocked, waited for Sue to answer, then entered. When the door shut, Bree took a steadying breath. Whatever he had gone to do, she told herself to be ready for anything. The Jack Walker she knew could reappear with an address book, a meat cleaver, or even Tyler himself. Nothing would surprise her. Not when it came to her father.

She checked her phone. No new texts from 555, but there was a voicemail notification from her mother. Not good. She quickly stuffed the phone back into her pocket (out of sight; out of mind) and told herself that was for later. She could only deal with one parent at a time.

She peered down the hallway. It already felt like her father had been gone too long, even though she knew it hadn't even been a minute. The air conditioning was barely moving the air, and light perspiration had broken on her face and arms. There was also a smell she hadn't noticed before: perfumes or lotions or maybe one of those plug-in air fresheners. Whatever it was, it was enough to make her stomach churn, and all at once the apartment felt too small, too warm, and she positioned herself by the front door, wanting nothing more than to bolt, but knowing she wouldn't. Couldn't. A few more minutes and this would all be over. A few more minutes and she would never have to come back here. Never have to see her father again.

Her gaze drifted into the kitchen and came to an abrupt stop on the refrigerator. Two items were pinned to the front: the scribblings of a grocery list and a tattered photograph with curled corners. It wasn't until she took a step closer that she actually believed what she was seeing: Tyler, her, and Alissa as kids, posing in front of a bank of pinball machines at McAtee's Pizza. Tyler was maybe nine, and Alissa was in Bree's arms, almost too big to hold. It had been a family outing for their mother's birthday, and each of them had been given a pocketful of quarters to play video games. Tyler, always looking for fresh ways to win their mother's affections, had immediately sought out the claw machine in the hopes of winning her a stuffed bear. Bree remembered it like it was yesterday…

"Once Mom sees this bear," Tyler said, "it's gonna make those earrings you got her at the dollar store look like puke."

Bree made a grunt of acknowledgement, scarcely listening. She'd been watching her parents for most of the night, and even at age fourteen, she knew something was off.

"Do you think Mom's… happy?" she asked Tyler, looking over her shoulder at her parents, who were huddled together in a booth—not in an intimate way, but more of a "trying to hide what was being said" way.

"I don't know," Tyler said shortly, clearly more concerned with maneuvering the claw than answering questions. "Why the shit-hell wouldn't she be?"

Tyler had recently discovered profanity and used it at every possible opportunity, and in every ridiculous combination, but never within earshot of their parents.

"What's a shit-hell?" Alissa asked. Bree hadn't realized Alissa had left the television in the corner where her face had been pressed, mesmerized, for the last fifteen minutes.

"Assballs!" Tyler cried, slapping a hand against the front of the machine. He shot Alissa a sideways glance as he fed another quarter into the machine. "Don't distract me. And don't repeat what I say. And go away."

"Take my quarters," Bree said, passing them to Alissa, whose eyes lit up in delight. "Go play that clown game that gives you tickets if you win."

Alissa dashed off, pigtails bouncing. When Bree looked back at the booth, their mother was crying.

"Hey," Bree whispered fiercely, tugging at Tyler's shirt. "I think—"

"I almost had one!" Tyler said. He glowered at Bree. "Do you know how hard this is? I only have two more quarters left, so stop... bothering... me."

Bree didn't need to be told twice, but only because their mother had escaped the booth and was making her way into the women's bathroom. Bree's head swung back and forth between her mother and father, and when her father caught her eye, his lips drew back in a grimace before he slid out of the booth and went off in the opposite direction.

Bree made her way toward the bathroom, weaving past kids and parents, hearing only her pulse in her ears. When she pushed through the bathroom door she found her mother at the sink, dabbing her cheeks with paper towels and trying (and failing) to not smudge her eyeliner.

"Mom?"

Her mother clapped her hand to her chest. "Bree," she said with a stunted laugh, "you can't creep up on people like that. If I was a cat, I'd be down to eight lives."

"I'm sorry," Bree said, all at once feeling guilty, even though she knew she wasn't doing anything wrong. "I saw you and Dad... talking. Is everything okay?"

"Of course. You know your dad: Mr. Grumpy when he hasn't gotten enough sleep, and he doesn't sleep well when he's worried. But he knows as well as I do that contractors are always looking for people with construction experience, and he'll find another job soon. It's not like we're going to be tossed out onto the street. That doesn't happen to real people. Not people with families and friends in their lives like us."

Her mother checked herself in the mirror, tossed the paper towels into the garage, and gave Bree a pinched smile.

"Don't you spend one second worrying about this, Bree. If I have to find a second job in the meantime, I can do that. I can always waitress in the evenings and on the weekends. My mother did it, and my grandmother did it, and I bet you dollars to doughnuts that my great-grandmother also waitressed. It's honest work, and if it was good enough for them, it's good enough for me."

The bathroom door swung open, and a teenage girl with cropped hair and incisors the size of ice cubes squeezed past and closed herself into the far bathroom stall. Bree's mother dropped a hand to the back of Bree's neck, then bent down and pressed a kiss to her forehead. Bree knew that was the end of it. For now. Until next month. Or next week.

"Come on," she told Bree. "Your father is waiting. And I suspect your brother is trying to win me a stuffed animal, so let's go cheer him on. It's so sweet of him to spend those quarters on me. I might even have a few more at the bottom of my purse for him. It's important that we celebrate the small victories. We may not have a lot, but we have each other, and that's the most important thing. Always remember that family sticks together... no matter what."

"Bree?"

Bree blinked, lifted her head. Her father was holding out a scrap of cigarette carton with what looked to be an address written across the inside.

"Tyler was here a few weeks ago," he told her. He spoke slowly, wrestling the words from his mouth. "He was as skittish as an alley cat, and his knuckles were raw and bruised. He didn't say what happened, and I didn't ask. Sue got his phone number and the address of where he was staying so we could stay in touch, but he made it clear not to share it if someone came looking for him." Her father leveled his gaze at her. "I would have never guessed that someone would be you."

"It's not like that," Bree said. "I'm trying to help him."

"Are you?"

Bree didn't meet his eyes. The honest truth was, she didn't know. Alissa's abductor hadn't directly said he was going to hurt Tyler, but it was clear that was the intent. And did Bree really expect Tyler to willingly go to his fate when she found him and explained everything? It wasn't like she could knock him over the head and drag him there. Her best chance was that Tyler knew who was doing this, and the two of them could find Alissa with no one getting hurt. That was how it was going to happen. She was sure of it. And she almost believed that.

Her father made no motion to hand over the address. Bree itched to reach out and take it, but she knew better than to try to take something that hadn't yet been offered. That lesson had been learned the hard way, and Bree still had the cigarette burn scar on her wrist to prove it.

"I don't know what Tyler has gotten himself into," he said, "but I know you can fix it. You've always been strong. Capable." He gave her a grave nod. "I did a piss-poor job of taking care of our family, but it makes me proud to see you take charge. Family is more important than anything. You and Tyler always remember that. Watch out for each other."

"And Alissa?" Bree asked.

It slipped out before she could catch herself. She wasn't sure if it was a question, a comment, or a challenge. She waited for him to react, to say something—*anything*—but his face remained impassive as he handed her the address.

"Thanks," she mumbled, shoving it into her pocket. "I gotta—"

"That picture on the fridge," he said. "It was taken at that one pizza place you kids liked, but I don't remember the name." His tone was mild, almost resigned. "Do you remember going there?"

"No," Bree answered flatly, opening the door. "I don't."

"Bree."

She turned, and before she could ask what he wanted, he pulled her into a bear hug that threatened to collapse her ribs. The smell of his aftershave sent a wave of emotions flooding through her, and then she was free, and her father was walking down the hallway into the bedroom, leaving Bree standing alone at the front door on the verge of unwanted tears.

CHAPTER SIX

It had taken almost a full minute for Bree to compose herself before leaving the apartment, and another few minutes once she was inside her truck. By the time she pulled into the first gas station she found, her adrenaline had retreated into a pulsing headache, and her father's face was a fading memory. Now she had to hope her father had been on the level. The phone number he had given her had been disconnected, and there was no way to know if Tyler would still be at that address—*if* he even had been in the first place. And if he wasn't, Bree wasn't sure what she would do. But that wasn't her immediate concern. Her truck was running on fumes, and if she didn't put some gas in the tank, she wouldn't be going anywhere.

"Shit."

She swiped her debit card again and saw the same message: DECLINED. But was she really that surprised? One of Bree's main contributions to the family was weekly groceries, and even with her employee discount, it didn't take much to drain her meager bank account. Because it wasn't just food she was purchasing: it was cleaning supplies, toiletries, underwear, and socks… The items were endless. Two weeks ago, Alissa had talked Bree into buying a stainless steel water bottle that cost almost twenty dollars. Bree fretted silently about it for hours afterward, but she also hated that they couldn't be spontaneous with purchases. She hated that Alissa (like her) was always denied when it came to buying nice things or doing things like going on trips, or going out to eat. She hated that the towels in their bathroom were old and threadbare, that the majority of their clothing shopping was done at discount retail stores or thrift shops, where Bree would joke about how they were being kitsch or ironic or retro, when they both knew it was because they were poor and one step above food stamps.

Bree checked her pockets for cash, knowing she had none, but was still frustrated when she came up empty. There were a few coins in the truck's ashtray, but those wouldn't be enough for even a gallon of gas. According to her phone's GPS, Tyler's address was no more than a few miles away, but if she ran out of gas, she was screwed. There was no backup plan. No one to call to save the day. There was only her. And that meant she couldn't leave this station without gasoline in her tank.

She looked through the storefront. The clerk was a young kid, maybe even high-school age, restocking cigarettes and paying her no notice. It would be easy enough to gas up and drive off without paying, but she couldn't risk getting caught. She had to try something more subtle. And as much as it disgusted her, she knew what she had to do. She knew how boys worked. How they thought. Just because she had no time for or interest in dating them, it didn't mean she was oblivious to their leers. Men's eyes had been following her since she had filled out in the ninth grade.

"Do what you have to do," she told herself, twisting the truck's side mirror upward to see the damage. It was worse than she feared: puffy eyes, smeared mascara, and splotchy cheeks. She fluffed her lifeless hair with a sigh and told herself men were all about the boobs anyway. At least she had a tight-fitting T-shirt going in her favor.

She crossed the parking lot and stepped through the sliding doors. The clerk barely glanced up as she approached the counter, and she plastered on the widest, most over-the-top flirtatious smile she could muster under the circumstances.

"Oh… my… gosh," she exclaimed, trying to project her best I'm-such-a-silly-girl tone, "but you are *not* going to believe this."

This was the part where the clerk was supposed to ask, "Believe what?" But he only regarded her with bored interest as he continued stocking cigarettes. She had misjudged his age (the wrinkles around his eyes suggested he was at least in his mid-twenties), and his delicate features—added to the fact that he was wearing more eyeliner than Alissa—didn't bode well for her plan to seduce gasoline.

"I forgot my purse at home," Bree explained, certain her cheeks were going to split open if she held her fake smile much longer. "My fuel gauge is on empty, and if I don't get at least a few gallons in the tank, I'm not going to make it back home, and I don't know what I'll do then."

The clerk had finally stopped stocking, but only because the cigarette carton in his hands was now empty. He began mechanically breaking down the cardboard, studying her, his face set like plaster. Bree was pretty sure he hadn't blinked once. She told herself to just turn and leave—there was no way this was going to happen.

"Look," she said with a heavy sigh, dropping all pretenses, "I really, *really* need some help right now. There's a situation happening, and I have to put gas in my truck. My sister's life depends on it."

It sounded ridiculous even to her ears. She dug out her driver's license and set it on the counter in front of him.

"This is me," she said. "Bree Walker. I'll leave my license here and come back tomorrow and pay for the gas then. If I was trying to scam you, would I show this to you and offer to leave it here? I just need—"

"Could be fake," the clerk said.

She was momentarily startled by the sound of his voice. "What do you mean 'fake'? It's my driver's license. That's me, right there."

"Sure, the picture is you, but that doesn't mean the name and address are yours. All that means"—he held up one hand before she could protest—"all it *could* mean is that you got a fake ID made, and now you're trying to con me."

There was no way she had just heard what she thought she had heard. "You're joking, right? You really think I paid hundreds of dollars for a fake ID just so I could hope to get twenty dollars' worth of gas? That's what you think?"

"Maybe," the clerk replied, working open another carton of cigarettes. "I never said you were a smart thief. And it's interesting that you know how much a fake ID costs. Who's to say you didn't con someone into making that for you and never paid them? Maybe you had it made for something else and you're figuring out new ways to use it. The girl barely looks like you, if you want to know the truth."

Bree snatched back her driver's license. The photo was from three years ago, and she had been a little heavier, and her hair had been curlier and darker, but it was unmistakably her.

"I'm sorry," the clerk said, not sounding sorry at all, "but if I set my better judgment aside for everyone who came here with a sob story, I'd be fired in a second. In the two years I've worked here, I've heard every excuse. A woman came in just last weekend and swore she purchased a winning fifty-dollar scratch-off lottery ticket, but she'd lost it, and 'couldn't I just be a good sport and give her the money anyway?'" He uttered an ugly, short laugh. "Like I said, I've seen and heard it all."

"But I'm not lying," Bree insisted. She tossed a hand toward the camera above the counter. "My face is being filmed, and I know it. If I was trying to cheat you, I wouldn't be okay with that. I will come back later and pay you. I promise."

He stared at her, his lips set in a thin line. He wasn't going to help. She could see it in his glazed-over eyes. Nothing she said or did was going to change his mind, and that meant she was back at square one, and that wasn't an option. For a horrible moment, she saw herself leaping over the counter, forcing him to turn on the pump, and demanding he lay face down on the ground while she filled her truck. No—she would take *money*, tie him up so he couldn't call the police, and drive to another gas station so she didn't linger at the scene of the crime. With a little luck, it would be hours before the clerk was discovered, and once she saved Alissa—and this ordeal was over—Bree would explain everything to the police.

It was a ridiculous plan, guaranteed to fail (even if she had the courage to try it), and it took everything inside her not to scream or explode. It must have shown, because for the first time since she stepped through the doors, there was a look of uncertainty on the clerk's face. The cigarette carton dipped in his hands as he drew away from the counter, his indifference edging toward apprehension. It was over. Bree told herself to leave, to go before he panicked and did something drastic like trip the silent alarm. But her feet refused to budge because there was nowhere for her to go; it was do or die time, and something was about to happen. And whatever that something was, she knew it was going to happen *fast*.

She opened her mouth, unsure what was about to come out, when the sliding doors behind her dinged. Bree was dumbfounded to see Liz.

"What are you doing here?" Bree stammered. Through the storefront she could see Liz's yellow moped parked behind her truck. "You followed me?"

Liz shot a tentative glance at the clerk as she took two steps inside. "I told you, I can help. You need my help. I'm not going to sit on my hands and do nothing."

Bree started to protest and then all at once realized Liz was right: she could help.

"Do you have any money?" Bree asked.

"What?"

Bree advanced on Liz with such velocity that Liz staggered backward two steps in surprise. "Money," Bree repeated. "You want to help? This is how you help."

The apprehension on Liz's face now rivaled that of the clerk's. Liz's eyes stayed on Bree as she dipped into her back pocket, hesitated, and pulled out a crumpled wad of bills. Bree snatched them up and slapped them on the counter.

"Here," she said, smoothing out the bills and praying they weren't all singles. "This is for gas on pump…" She shot a glance over her shoulder. "Whatever pump my truck is parked beside."

There were four singles, one five, and a ten with a torn corner. Nineteen dollars. It was enough. The clerk only gawked at the money from the far side of the counter, and a realization rose inside Bree: he wasn't going to take it. He wanted nothing to do with this and wanted Bree out of the store as quickly as possible—money or no money.

"I'm sorry," Bree said, doing her best to soften her tone. "I shouldn't have come in here and put you in the awkward position of helping me and then getting upset when you couldn't. I'm sick out of my mind with worry right now, and the fastest way for you to get me out of your store is to take this money, put it in your register, and turn on the pump. Please. I'm begging you." Bree's voice had become a painful croak. "Help me help my sister. You can even keep some of the money for yourself if you want. Even ten dollars in gas would get me where I need to go. Please…"

The clerk's eyes narrowed, assessing her. He *still* wasn't going to help her. Even now. A tremor of anger swept through Bree, but before she could speak, the clerk took the money from the counter.

"Nineteen dollars on pump two," he said. "And this is the last time you step foot inside this gas station. Either of you."

"Thank you," Bree said. She grabbed Liz by the arm and led her out of the store.

"Well?" Liz asked as they crossed the parking lot.

Bree released Liz, unscrewed the gas cap, and heaved the nozzle into her truck. "Well, what?"

"Did you find out where Tyler is?"

"Maybe," Bree answered shortly. The pump hadn't started yet, and Bree leaned forward and saw the clerk watching them through the storefront. Bree tossed an impatient hand in the air and motioned for the clerk to get things going.

"What did your dad say when you told him about Alissa?" Liz asked.

Bree's chest went tight. "What do you mean?"

"I know your dad lives there. So does Alissa. Tyler told us."

Bree pursed her lips. Of course Alissa knew. She knew because Tyler knew. Within the last few years, Tyler and Alissa had become as thick as thieves. Almost conspiratorial. Bree hadn't asked for the job of co-parenting her siblings, but that was how things had played out, and the older Alissa got, the more Tyler became the fun, carefree sibling who was always quick with a joke or a wild story, while Bree remained the uptight sibling who nagged and sucked the fun out of everything.

"We went there last month," Liz said, "after I got my moped. I told Alissa it wasn't a good idea, but she begged me."

Bree was almost afraid to ask. "Was our father... Did he see Alissa?"

Liz dropped her gaze. It was answer enough.

"He refused to see her," Bree said in a thin voice. She wasn't sure if it was anger or anguish she was feeling. "Is that what happened?"

Liz gave a half shrug. "A woman answered the door. She said your dad wasn't home. She was nice. It sounded like she felt really bad about what she was saying. Before she finished talking, Alissa left down the stairs, and by the time I caught up to her outside, she was crying."

Bree didn't want to hear the rest.

"Alissa said she heard a door open in the inside hallway when we were talking, and she could see a shadow on the hallway floor, like someone was standing there, listening. And maybe it wasn't him. Maybe someone else was there, visiting or something. I tried to tell Alissa that, but…"

Bree could see it in her mind's eye: big, brave Jack Walker, cowering in the hallway, listening to every word just out of sight, because that was what he did. He didn't face the world like a man; he hid from it. Just on the edge. Just enough to feel like he still kept his dignity.

Bree's phone dinged. It was a message from their mother:

Is Alissa back at home? She's not answering her phone.

Bree stared at the screen. This wasn't good. Ignoring a voicemail was one thing, but ignoring a text was something else. If Bree didn't respond, her mother would call again, only this time she wouldn't be content to leave a voicemail. No, her mother would call over and over, continuously, repeatedly, for as long as it took for Bree to pick up. In her mother's mind, if the Walker girls weren't answering their phones or replying to messages, it was because they were out doing something they weren't supposed to be doing, like participating in violent orgies, or ingesting drugs. Bree texted back:

Working on it.

The message sent. Bree had always been a lousy liar, and if her mother called to ask why Alissa wasn't home yet—or why Alissa wasn't responding to texts and phone calls—Bree didn't know what she would say or do. Bree could only hope her mother wouldn't use her own phone's GPS (like she had done many times before) to track Alissa's location, because if she saw it was disabled, it would send her mother into full panic mode, possibly even enough to contact the police.

The texting bubble appeared on Bree's screen, and time slowed to a nauseating crawl as Bree waited for the response. The pump kicked on, giving Bree a start.

"What are they texting you?" Liz asked.

"It's my mother," Bree replied absently.

"We have to tell her," Liz said. "She can help us."

"I already told you, we can't—"

Bree's phone rang, sending her stomach into a slow, forward roll. Her mother had abandoned the text and was calling. There was no avoiding it now. She took a deep breath as she raised the phone to her ear.

"Hi, Mom."

"Am I bad mother?" were the first words out of her mother's mouth. "I must be, because if I had raised my girls right, one of them would have returned my texts or answered their phone when I called over my coffee break. But instead, here I am, hiding in the bathroom to sneak a call on my cell phone, because there are no more coffee breaks for me. So I'm the one who's sorry, Bree. I have clearly failed my children."

Bree knew better than to speak. She knew how this worked. Her mother was having a horrible night and someone had to bear the brunt of it. Her mother would rant, Bree would listen, and then they would move past it onto the next order of business.

"This might be my worst night ever," her mother said, as she had said a hundred times before. "The new busboy quit after only an hour; Cindy called in sick again; and the full moon is bringing in every redneck weirdo this side of town. I just had a customer cram a dollar bill into the pocket of my apron like I was some cheap pole dancer or stripper. If he hadn't been on his way out, I would have asked Karl to boot him. Not that Karl would have. He never does when I ask. He would if Jenny asked him. But not me. *Never* for me."

"I'm sorry, Mom," Bree said. The numbers on the pump continued to creep along—just under two gallons now.

"I don't know how much longer I can do this, Bree. Something has got to give. Something has got to change. My reserves are running low, and I don't see a vacation in my future, only more double shifts and more sleazy customers. Is it too much to ask for even a weekend off? Just one? Two glorious days of nothing but sitting with my feet up with a good book?" Her mother let out a sigh that seemed to last forever. "I'm sorry. For real. It's been a night, and I shouldn't take it out on you, but I know you get it. Alissa's home now, like I asked?"

Three gallons now. "Yes."

"Good. Make sure she straightens up the living room and folds the bathroom towels. And everything is good between you two now?"

"Yes."

There was silence from the other end. Her mother knew something was wrong. She could sense it in Bree's tone. Mother's intuition, whatever you wanted to call it. And now, in the next few seconds, all of this would be out of Bree's hands, because once her mother knew the truth of what had happened, she would call the police and the machinery would be in motion, and that would be that. Alissa's fate would be out of Bree's hands, and maybe that would be for the best.

"I know Alissa is going through the 'terrible teens' right now," her mother said, "but like the 'terrible twos,' it will pass. Alissa needs you. She may not know it, and she may not show it, but she does. These last few months have been extremely difficult for Alissa because of what happened, but we'll all get through it."

Because of what happened. That was putting it mildly. The worst part was that their mother still blamed herself, no matter how much Bree tried to convince her otherwise. What their mother had done was a forgivable mistake; what their father had done—and continued to do—was not.

"I should go," Bree said as the pump kicked off. "I should make sure Alissa doesn't need anything."

Her mother cleared her throat, and Bree could only imagine what was coming next. "I don't have to go into work until four on Sunday, so we're going to sit down and have a nice family lunch. You, me, Alissa, and Tyler. It's been way too long since he's been home. I want all my babies under my roof at the same time, even for just one meal. We can do that, can't we?"

"Yes."

"Good. We don't have to talk about anything important. We can just enjoy being a family. I think Tyler switched phones again, and I don't have his new number, so I'll leave that to you. You can get his number from one of his friends, right? You always seem to know how to get in touch with him. Tell him to be at our house by noon. And Bree? Be good to Alissa. You only have one sister. Believe it or not, you were once young and reckless and did impetuous things. Do I need to remind you about the time you and Anisha Thurlow tried to straighten your hair using my steam iron? Or when the two of you thought it would be fun to hang onto the back of passing cars while wearing roller skates? You still have a small scar on your knee from that act of brilliance, if I remember correctly. And…" All at once her mother's voice was muffled, as if she had lowered the phone and was speaking to someone else. "Bree. I have to get back. I'll see you when I get home."

The phone clicked in Bree's ear. She pocketed it and jerked open the driver-side door.

"What did she say?" Liz asked.

"Nothing," Bree said, climbing into the truck. "I'm not telling you again, Liz: go home. You have no idea what you're getting yourself into."

"I don't care. If you don't let me come with you, then I'll just keep following on my moped."

"This isn't a game—"

"I know that!" Liz's voice was rife with anger. "And I'm not going to mess up and let Alissa get hurt again!"

"Again? What do you mean *again*?"

"Nothing," Liz answered sharply, but her chalky face told a different story. "That's between me and Alissa."

"And what happens to my family," Bree said evenly, "is between me and my family. I can't also be responsible for you."

Bree climbed into the truck, started the engine, and spied Liz through the rearview mirror. Liz remained motionless, and Bree could only imagine what was going through her head. Liz, unlike Alissa, had grit and determination and had already battled her way onto two honor rolls, earned a spot on the varsity volleyball team as a freshman, and had been working since age fourteen at Arant's Pet Palace. None of that changed anything. Bree couldn't— *wouldn't*—be responsible for Liz on top of everything else.

Bree took out the scrap of cardboard her father had given her and entered 72 Hempel Drive into her phone's GPS. Seven miles. If the address was right, Tyler was no more than ten minutes away.

"If I tell you what happened," Liz said, appearing at the driver-side window, "will you let me help?"

"No," Bree said. "I won't."

She dropped the truck into gear and sped off without looking back.

CHAPTER SEVEN

Bree rang the bell at 72 Hempel Drive again. The windows were shut, and the only indication of life was the continued barking from the adjoining half of the duplex. The dog had started the moment Bree had parked and crossed the lawn. Through the window, she could see from its massive size that its lung capacity wouldn't give out anytime soon. Whoever lived there surely had to hear the dog going nuts. Before Bree's family had moved into the trailer, they had briefly lived in a duplex (or townhouse, or zero lot line, or whatever they were called back then), and the shared wall between them had been notoriously thin. To make matters worse, the driveway was one large slab of concrete instead of two distinct, separate slabs, and even though it was made for two cars, their neighbor would continuously take up the whole slab, either because he was oblivious or because he simply didn't care. This would enrage Bree's father to no end, and more than once their "discussions" over it had almost come to blows. In Jack's younger days, their mother had always been able to calm Jack down—usually by distracting him with a cold beer or appealing to his ego, because surely tussling over something as insignificant as parking was "beneath" someone like Jack Walker, wasn't it? Not to mention the fact that their neighbor was in his mid-sixties and would clearly be no match for Jack. When it came to keeping the peace back then, their mother had been the only person their father listened to.

Bree knocked loudly on the screen door, and the barking abruptly stopped, either coincidentally or because some unseen neighbor had led the dog away from the window. Whatever the case, it was eerily quiet now, save for the light wind rustling the trees. And then, faintly within the duplex: footsteps. Louder with each step, as if the owner was climbing a set of wooden stairs. Bree straightened as the footsteps reached the door. There was the snick of a lock being disengaged, then another, before the door swung inward on a thin woman in her late thirties—*maybe* early forties—wearing a black tank top, no bra, with sinewy arms covered in faded tattoos of flowers. Her shoulder-length hair was the color of murky dishwater, and her skull nose ring was as inviting as the scowl on her lips.

"I don't donate to fundraisers," the woman said, "and I'm not looking for any amazing cleaning products, and I don't plan to vote this year, and I absolutely have no interest in joining your church. So… are we done here?"

Despite the woman's scowl, her tone was oddly amicable, as if she had given the speech a hundred times before to her own amusement. When Bree, momentarily caught off guard, didn't reply right away, the woman shrugged and started to close the door.

"I'm looking for Tyler Walker," Bree blurted out.

The door stopped. Before Bree could say anything more, the woman pushed open the screen door, forcing Bree backward a few steps. She was a few inches taller than Bree, smelled like weed, and was wearing bright-pink sandals that matched her shorts. Her eyes crawled suspiciously over Bree as she took a long drag from a slender, brown cigarette.

"Tyler Walker," the woman repeated. She turned her head, but only slightly, as she exhaled a lungful of smoke. Her eyes never left Bree. "Is he supposed to live here or something? Is that what you think? Someone tell you that?"

"I don't care if he lives here or just occasionally visits, or even if he just frequents your toilet. I need to talk to him. Is he here?"

"See, here's the problem," the woman said, tapping her ashes. "You're asking these questions, but I don't know who you are, or why you're knocking on my door, looking for him."

Bree felt her patience slip. "It's important that I talk to him."

"If you say so," the woman said with an indifferent shrug. "But that still doesn't change the fact that I don't know who you are, or why you're knocking on my door, or why you're looking for him."

"It's private," Bree said, all at once aware a pimply-faced teenage boy was watching from the open window on the other side of the duplex. "I was told Tyler is staying here with his girlfriend. Can I talk with her?"

"You can and are."

Bree made an involuntary grimace. "*You're* Tyler's girlfriend?"

The woman's grin flattened. "You're really something, you know that? You come here, disturb me from my work, you *still* haven't told me who you are, and now you have the nerve to make a comment like that?" She flicked her lit cigarette at Bree, who yelped in surprise when it bounced off her shoulder. "Yeah," the woman said brusquely, "we're *definitely* done here."

The woman started back inside, and Bree caught the screen door before it fully closed.

"Tyler's my brother," she said, "and if I don't find him, our sister is going to die. This isn't a joke."

The woman's head turned but only halfway. Bree's hand was squeezing the knob of the screen door hard enough to turn her knuckles white.

"What the hell am I supposed to say to that?" the woman asked. She swung around to face Bree, her face a taut mask. "You can't just throw out a comment like that on someone you don't know. What am I supposed to do with that? If I say I don't believe you, I'm an asshole bitch. But why *should* I believe you? Just because you say you know Tyler? Tyler knows a lot of people."

"If you don't want to believe I'm his sister, that's fine, but it doesn't change the fact that I'm telling you the truth. Our sister's name is Alissa. She's sixteen. And she's scared and alone, and she doesn't deserve this." Bree's voice rose in desperation. "If I could trade places with her, I'd do it in a heartbeat. But I can't. All I can do is find Tyler, my *brother*, who has tattoos up and down both arms, just like you. His hair is always buzzed to the length of his five o'clock shadow, and he's skinny but muscular and walks with a swagger, like he owns the goddamn world. It's not going to cost you a thing to let me talk to him, because you clearly know him, so why are we still standing here wasting time?"

Bree was breathing faster now, fighting to maintain her last bit of composure.

"That was a mouthful of information there," the woman told Bree. "I'm going to repeat it back to you now, just to make sure we're both on the same page. First, I'm supposed to believe Tyler is your brother because you described what he looks like. Second, if you don't find Tyler, then your sister is going to somehow die. Did I get that right?"

"Yes," Bree replied shortly, heat filling her cheeks.

"You left out the *why*."

Bree faltered. "What do you mean?"

"Why?" the woman repeated. "Why is Tyler the only one who can help your sister? Did she run away and Tyler's the only one who knows where she went? Is your sister in the hospital, and she needs a kidney transplant? Does she need Tyler's blood? Is Tyler the only one in town with her matching blood type?" The woman arched her eyebrows and crossed her arms as she leaned back. "You know what I think? I think that you're an old girlfriend looking to settle a score. I also think that *you* think I'm an idiot. Why else would you make up such a ridiculous story instead of keeping it simple? Why not just say you're pregnant or something? That's more believable."

"I'm telling you the truth—"

"No," the woman replied bluntly, "you're not. And I'll thank you to get off my porch now, because I'd like to get back to my basement to finish what I was doing. So go away and have a nice day."

Panic welled inside Bree as the front door began to close.

"Wait," Bree said, pulling open the screen door again. The woman burst back outside savagely enough to startle Bree backward down the steps.

"You want to try me?" the woman asked. Her eyes were locked on Bree, black and blazing. "I *was* going to hit the gym later today, but I have no problem doing my workout on you."

Bree held her ground, adrenaline coursing through her veins. "I didn't come here for this. I came here for my brother. You don't want to believe me, *fine*. But if you get Tyler—if you tell him my name, and tell him I'm here—I know he'll come out and talk to me. None of this has anything to do with you."

"But that's where you're wrong." The woman's face relaxed, but only slightly. "I've worked long and hard to build a life in this town, and I've fought to make this house my home. To keep the people I know and love safe. So you coming here *is* my business. And I know, on some level, you can understand and respect that. I can see it in your eyes. You've been through worlds of shit, same as me. Life hasn't easily given either of us what we have. We've had to take it." She lowered her head. "So I'm telling you, for the last time, whatever you came here to do, it isn't going to happen. I know that's a hard pill to swallow, but that's the way it has to be, and there's nothing else to say."

The woman disappeared inside without another word, leaving Bree alone in the yard. Bree started up the steps, stopped, turned away from the house, stopped, and all at once deflated. She tried to catch her thoughts. Arrange them. Tyler was inside, she was sure of it. So why hadn't he come out? Even with the windows closed, the front door had been open, and Tyler surely would have overheard the entire conversation. But the woman had said she wanted to get back to her basement. If she had been down there before answering the door, wasn't it possible that Tyler was also downstairs, watching television, or even listening to music, oblivious to what had happened? Bree had to believe that. As insensitive and apathetic as Tyler could be at times, he wouldn't intentionally ignore a plea for help—especially when it involved Alissa. Bree had to figure out what to do next. Because if Tyler wasn't inside...

She shook the thought from her head, not wanting to follow it through to its conclusion. It was futile and dangerous to speculate on things out of your control, or things that *might* happen. The human mind was quick to conjure up horrible images and scenarios based on nothing, and once she started down that road, it would emotionally cripple her. She couldn't allow that to happen. She had a job to do. First and foremost: getting inside this house. There was no backup plan. Tyler was either inside or he wasn't. And if he wasn't, then she would figure out what to do next. Knock on every door in town if she had to. Check every alley and parking lot. Track down Tyler's friends and acquaintances.

The pimply boy was back in the window on the other side of the duplex, trying (and failing) to watch without being seen. The entire left half of his face was visible, and as soon as he realized he was spotted, he ducked back out of sight.

Bree moved to the window, having no idea if Tyler's girlfriend was still watching or even if the pimply boy's mother or father was home and would question why a twenty-six-year-old woman was peeking inside their duplex. It was a calculated risk, but Bree was out of ideas.

The window was eye level and easy to see inside. The boy was near the corner, pressed against his closet door, eyes wide and holding his breath. He couldn't have been more than thirteen.

"I'm sorry," the boy said quickly, "my mom always says I shouldn't spy on people, and I don't mean to spy on people, but sometimes I just look out the window and people are there when I'm looking out, and then I keep looking, but I don't realize I'm looking, but I am—"

"It's okay," Bree said. "I used to do the same thing when I was your age. I'd spend hours staring out my window and watching the neighbors come and go, making up stories in my head about what they were doing and where they were going. Are you here alone?"

The boy gave a tentative nod. "My mom and dad are out running errands. I don't have any brothers or sisters; just Levi, our dog. I let him out into the backyard. He doesn't like people very much, so when he wouldn't stop barking at you, I put him in the backyard."

"I understand. Do you know the woman who lives on the other side?"

"Well… yeah. Maggie's lived there for a long time. As long as we have."

Bree lowered her voice. "Is there a guy that also stays there? Someone who looks around my age, maybe a little younger? Tattoos all over his arms, like Maggie? Short hair?"

"That's him. He's been coming around for a while now. I've never talked to him, but I've seen him, and he sometimes gives me a wave."

"Have you seen him today?" Bree asked.

"No, but I don't see him every day. He always comes and goes using the back door. I've never seen him in the front yard. I think he's trying to be sneaky. He always looks around a lot before he goes inside."

Bree's mind worked feverishly, trying to formulate a plan. "Do you ever go there and visit?"

"Do I ever go next door?" The boy peeled himself from the wall and warily approached the window. "No way. Maggie hates visitors. She doesn't even wave at me when I walk right past her when I'm coming home from school. She never says hello or hi or anything."

That wasn't the answer Bree wanted. The boy had been her best and only idea... but maybe she wasn't sunk yet.

"I'm going to level with you," Bree told him. "No bullshit. Are you listening?"

The boy was inches from the screen now, his face grave. "I'm listening."

"I need to get inside Maggie's house. It's a matter of life and death. I need you to knock on Maggie's door, tell her there's a problem over here—a water leak or something—and get her to leave and come check it out. Then I can stick my head inside the house and look for my brother."

The boy was nodding. "Yeah... no way I'm doing that."

For a moment, Bree thought she hadn't heard him correctly. "Wait. You're saying you *won't* do that?"

"No way I'm doing that. I'm not allowed to walk on any part of her yard. A few weeks ago, Levi got off his leash and pooped by Maggie's mailbox, and Maggie picked it up and smeared it all over our window screen." He raised his finger. "Right there. Right in front of where the tip of your nose is there."

Bree instinctively pulled away from the screen. The boy began backing away toward the bedroom door.

"What are you doing?" Bree asked.

"I'm gonna go watch TV in the other room now. I probably shouldn't tell my mom and dad about this, and you should probably leave before they come back. They don't like me talking to people I don't know."

"But—"

The boy was already gone through the door. Bree retreated to the sidewalk, more determined than ever now to get inside Maggie's. The boy was definitely bizarre, but she didn't see any reason why he would be lying about seeing Tyler there. Bree needed a plan, and she needed one fast.

Movement caught Bree's eye from across the street, and it only took a moment to spot Liz on her moped, trying to conceal herself behind a parked car, and not doing a very good job of it.

"Son of a bitch," Bree said under her breath.

As soon as Liz saw Bree coming, she dismounted, clenched her teeth, and stood her ground. "I'm not leaving," Liz said, speaking in rapid bursts, "because if anything happens to Alissa I'll never forgive myself. I owe her because she tried to kill herself!"

The words stopped Bree dead in her tracks. "*What?*"

"It happened last week when you and your mom were at work. It was because of Derek."

Bree could feel her lips moving, trying to form syllables, sentences, questions—make *any* sound—but her tongue had shriveled inside her mouth.

"Derek is a senior at our school," Liz said, "and he's a jerk who only wanted one thing from Alissa, and I tried to warn her about him, but she wouldn't listen—"

"Wait," Bree said, fighting to keep up. "You're saying Alissa tried to kill herself because of a boy?"

Liz dropped her eyes. "He's on the football team. He's popular and all the girls in our class like him. But he has a reputation, and I told Alissa that, but she didn't listen. And when Alissa went to his house and wouldn't... *do* the things Derek wanted, he got angry and dumped her. Then he started spreading rumors about her. He made up lies about the things she had done with him. People at school started calling Alissa names and sending her nasty text messages. Someone wrote on her locker. Alissa freaked out, and I told her it was going to be okay, because her real friends knew she didn't do any of those things, but she wouldn't listen. She acted like this was somehow my fault and started getting mad at me, and I was only trying to help!"

Bree tried to think back to last week, tried to remember Alissa being more upset than normal. It had been a crazy week with their mother working double shifts (leaving early in the morning and not returning until late at night), with Bree putting in overtime to help with the annual grocery store inventory.

"I tried to be a good friend about it, but I *told* Alissa this was going to happen if she went out with him, and she should have listened. But she didn't, and then it was all she could talk about. And yeah, it sucked for her, but those same types of rumors spread about Rebecca Carson after Derek dumped her, and that blew over in a few weeks. And I kept trying to tell that to Alissa, but she wouldn't listen, and she kept sending me texts all hours of the night, and I finally told her to stop feeling sorry for herself and stop acting like it was the end of the world—because it wasn't—and she wasn't the only one who has problems, but she never wants to listen to mine."

Liz stared bleakly at Bree, shaking her head, eyes glistening with tears.

"I started ignoring Alissa's texts," Liz said in a hollow voice. "I couldn't do it anymore. I didn't want to be around her. I had my own stuff to deal with. We don't have any classes together this trimester, so it was easy to avoid her at school. I felt bad about it, but I knew she'd get over it, because all of her real friends knew the rumors weren't true…"

Bree's heart was a slow, heavy throb inside her chest as she waited for Liz to finish.

"I didn't hear from Alissa for a couple days," Liz said, "and then I got a text. It was just the word 'goodbye.' I was getting ready to go out of town with my dad, so I thought it was because of that. I texted Alissa back and told her I was sorry and that she should come over and say goodbye in person… but I never heard anything back." Liz looked at Bree through teary eyes. "I had a really bad feeling come over me. I couldn't get rid of it. I sent Alissa more texts, but I never heard anything. So I finally went over to your trailer... and..."

Bree swallowed what little saliva she had. "And?"

"Alissa didn't answer the front door, but it was unlocked, so I went inside. She wasn't in her room, but when I looked inside the bathroom..." Liz gave a gulping sob. "Alissa was lying on the floor, and I couldn't see her face, and at first I thought she was dead... but she wasn't. She was curled into a ball, staring at nothing. On the floor by her feet was an orange pill bottle. It was empty."

"Mom's high blood pressure medicine," Bree said, casting her mind back. Alissa had told their mother she had accidentally knocked the open pill bottle into the toilet, and all the pills had been flushed away. That had been last Tuesday... no, Wednesday, the night Bree had made spaghetti, Alissa's favorite meal. Alissa hadn't eaten any. She had stayed in her room all night, claiming she didn't feel well. Bree hadn't thought to connect the two things together. Why would she?

Liz was crying now, a soft, silent sound. "The pills made Alissa lightheaded and sick. She threw up in the bathtub. I cleaned it up. Then I cleaned Alissa up. I put her into her bed and stayed with her until your mom got home. I told your mom that Alissa and I had accidentally eaten some rotten eggs for breakfast and that made Alissa sick."

A car drove past, momentarily startling Bree. When she turned her attention back to Liz, tears were streaming down Liz's cheeks.

"Don't you see?" Liz asked. Her voice seared into Bree. "It was *my* fault Alissa tried to kill herself. If I had been there for her... if I hadn't just blown her off because I was annoyed, she wouldn't have done it. And it was just dumb luck that those pills weren't something that *could* kill her, but what if they had been? I didn't help Alissa that time until it was too late, but I can help her now, and I'm not going to mess up again, and... and... I..."

Liz's face collapsed into tears as she fell into Bree's arms, and all at once Bree was so overcome with emotion she had to fight for breath. She could see Alissa in her mind's eye, standing in the bathroom, clutching the pill bottle, staring at herself in the mirror and daring (hoping?) her reflection would reach through and stop her... but at the same time, knowing that one swallow would make everything go away. No more pain or uncertainty, only eternal sleep. Bree knew this because it wasn't Alissa that she was seeing in the mirror—it was herself at age fifteen, different mirror, different bathroom, same emotions.

"We're going to get Alissa," Bree said somberly, holding Liz steady. "Alissa wasn't hurt then, and she won't be hurt now. We'll get her. You and me."

Liz's head moved up and down, her face hot against Bree's neck. It could have been Alissa in her arms, and Bree lifted her head to hold back her tears.

CHAPTER EIGHT

"I'm home," Bree called out, tossing her truck keys onto the table. "Alissa and Liz, I have your frozen pizza and chips and ice cream."

She set the paper grocery sack on the counter and peered down the hallway. Alissa's bedroom door stood open, but the bathroom door was closed, which was always worrisome. Bree had only been gone a half hour, but it didn't take long for two twelve-year-old girls to get into trouble when left to their own devices—especially during a sleepover.

Bree drifted down the hallway and knocked on the bathroom door. "Girls? You in there? Everything okay?"

"Yes," Alissa replied curtly. "We're fine, so go away."

Not exactly the reassuring answer Bree was looking for. She tried the knob (in the Walker household, a crap attitude immediately forfeited your right to privacy), and found it locked.

"Open it," Bree said, knocking again. She knew it was probably nothing: boy troubles, or drama at school, or one (or both) of them had secretly gotten a tattoo that was now infected and would surely lead to a painful death within hours. "Right now, Alissa. Don't make me get the key."

The knob clicked and the door opened. Bree didn't really expect to see any boys or booze inside, but she still felt a sigh of relief when she saw only Liz sitting on the floor with her knees pulled into her chest, cheeks wet with tears. Alissa settled back onto the floor beside Liz and took her hand. Whatever the problem was, it clearly wasn't Alissa, so that was a plus. Bree couldn't count how many times their sleepovers had been cut short early over petty fights that ended up in tears. It was the curse of best friends.

"Is it an inside hurt or outside hurt?" Bree asked.

Alissa rolled her eyes. It was something Bree used to ask Alissa when she was younger: an "inside hurt" was anything from a tummy ache to hurt feelings, while an "outside hurt" meant a jammed finger or a scraped knee. Sometimes Bree forgot the girls weren't six any more although they often acted that age during sleepovers: giggling and shouting and chasing each other around the trailer. Chances were it was something emotional or hormonal seeing as there were no visible cuts or scrapes or blood...

"Oh," Bree said as the thought hit her. "Liz, is this your first... womanly thing?"

"Womanly thing?" Alissa asked for Liz, and before Bree could formulate a response, something in Alissa's face clicked, and her cheeks turned a hard red. "Ewww. No, it's nothing like that. Stop."

Bree shot Alissa a warning with her eyes—I'm only trying to help—before sitting on the closed toilet lid. Liz sniffled and rubbed her eyes with her palms.

"Do you want to talk about it?" Bree asked softly.

Liz gave a tentative shrug.

Bree waited a few seconds, and when nothing more was forthcoming, Bree stood with a resigned sigh. "Maybe it would be best for me to take Liz home—"

"No!" Liz cried. "Don't make me go!"

Bree cast an eye at Alissa, whose complexion had gone sickly white. It was obvious Alissa was trying to act tough and in control, but it was also clear that Alissa had no idea what to do. Whatever this was, Bree had walked right into the middle of it.

Liz was crying again, snot and tears collecting on her upper lip.

"It's going to be okay," Bree said, placing a gentle hand on Liz's head, stroking her hair. "Tell me what's wrong."

"She-she-she..." Liz swallowed and drew a frayed breath. "She doesn't want me."

Bree frowned. "Who doesn't want you?"

"My m-m-mom."

"Of course she does," Bree said automatically. "Why would you think that?"

"They're getting a divorce," Alissa answered for Liz. "Her mom moved out."

Bree's stomach sank. "Oh, honey... I'm so sorry."

Bree grasped for something more to say, but the only thing that came to mind was, "It's probably for the best." She didn't figure that would be helpful, even if it was the truth. Years of school functions, sleepover drop-offs, and first-hand encounters at the grocery store had reinforced how awful and abrasive Liz's mother could be, and that was nothing compared to the stories Alissa shared: Liz's mom locking Liz inside her bedroom at night; denying Liz school lunch money as a form of punishment; never celebrating (or even acknowledging) Liz's birthday. Liz's mother was the main reason Liz spent so much time at the Walker trailer, and a part of Bree would have guessed Liz would be happy about this development. But another part of Bree knew (from her own experience) that you only had one mother and father, and no matter how horrible they were, they were still your mother and father.

"Sometimes adults hurt inside," Bree said, choosing her words carefully, "and that hurt is deep and so intense that the person hurting doesn't know how to fix it. I think your mother is really unhappy, and that comes out in her words and actions. You mother is unhappy with herself, hon, not you. Deep down, she loves you. I know she does."

"She doesn't," Liz whispered.

"Now come on," Bree said, inserting some tough love as she squeezed Liz's shoulder. "You know that's not true—"

"She told me," Liz said, the anguish in her voice now laced with anger. "She told me she never wanted a kid, and she wasn't happy with her life, and she couldn't do this anymore. My mother told me that."

Liz stared at Bree, daring her to speak. Alissa had often accused Bree of having the empathy of a gnat, and maybe Alissa was right, because right now, at this moment, Bree had nothing, no words to make this better.

"She doesn't want me," Liz said in a teary voice, "and she doesn't love me, so don't lie and say she does, because we all know it's not true."

Liz scrambled up from the floor and pushed her way blindly out of the bathroom. A moment later, Alissa's bedroom door slammed shut.

"Thanks for making things worse," Alissa said, rising to her feet. "I told you not to come in here. I almost had her calmed down. Why can't you ever trust me?"

"I was only trying to help," Bree said. "I'm sorry."

Alissa was already in the hallway opening her bedroom door. Bree reached it just as it closed and put her hand to the knob, but didn't turn it. Through the thin wood she could hear Liz's choking sobs.

"Liz," Bree said, putting a hand to the door. "I'm so sorry…"

Bree closed her eyes. When she reopened them, Alissa's bedroom door was gone, and in its place was Bree's truck. Liz was sixteen again, standing on the sidewalk across from Bree, her face red and blotchy, still struggling to compose herself as Bree replayed Liz's story over and over in her head, feeling worse each time. Because Bree did remember that night—sitting on Alissa's bed, stroking Alissa's hair, trying to get her to open up because she suspected more was going on than just an upset stomach. And when Alissa's head had peeked out from the blankets, there had been a long, drawn-out, hopeful moment where Bree thought Alissa was going to tell her everything, and things would be like they were before, when Alissa came to Bree with her problems, whether it was trouble at school, a fight with a friend, or even to complain about the family. Bree missed the little girl who was afraid to sleep alone at night and would sneak Bree's pillows into her bunk bed in the hopes Bree would sleep below her. The girl who would snuggle on the couch for hours while they watched Saturday morning cartoons, who loved helping make dinner, whether it was assembling tacos, stirring scrambled eggs, or layering lasagna noodles into the pan.

They were a team… until junior high happened. Instead of Alissa moving Bree's pillows at bedtime, she shut her bedroom door on Bree, and just like that, Alissa's sleeping issues were vanquished. It was the beginning of the end. One day Bree was needed, wanted, and the most important person in Alissa's life… and then she wasn't. And as the days turned into weeks and months and years, and Alissa chose activities and friends over Bree, Bree's heart had slowly hardened—not because she wanted it that way, but because it was the only way to protect herself. She had never been especially close with her mother or father or brother, but Alissa had been different. Alissa had given her purpose. Someone to love. Someone to watch out for.

"I'm sorry," Liz said. "I should have told you sooner. Even before tonight. I should have told you when it happened, but Alissa begged me not to, and since she was already mad at me, and since I already felt so terrible about it, I told her I'd keep it a secret."

Bree nodded, hating the twinge of resentment she felt toward Liz, knowing it was unfounded. There was no way Liz could have known what Alissa might do. Girls fought, and they were petty, and sometimes they just didn't think. Bree had ignored her best friend her entire freshman year of high school over a boy. Or maybe it was over something that happened at a sleepover or at summer camp. Bree couldn't even remember now. How pathetic was that?

"You really think Tyler's in there?" Liz asked.

Bree peered through the large row of pine trees between them and the duplex. "He's in there. I'm sure of it. But since his girlfriend isn't going to let me inside, we need to get her outside. And once she's out, I can go in and get Tyler. I just need one second to make contact with him. Once I do that, we can figure out the rest."

"How do we get her to come outside?"

Bree wet her lips as the wheels began to turn. "We give her a reason. We tell her something happened. Something bad, like an accident. There's been an accident and someone was hurt, and that person needs help."

Liz looked over her shoulder into the street. "But… there isn't an accident. And she'll see there isn't."

"That's because it happened on the next street over. The accident can't be seen from here. You need to *take* her to the accident."

"But wouldn't she just call for an ambulance? Why would she come with me? And if the accident is on the next street over, why would I walk all the way over to this house? Why wouldn't I just go to the first house I saw?"

Bree's jaw tightened, but Liz had a point.

"A flat tire," Bree said. "You have a flat tire on your moped and you ask if she can come and help you fix it. Or maybe it's just low on air, and you need a tire pump."

Bree realized all the flaws before Liz started shaking her head.

"What if she doesn't have a tire pump?" Liz asked. "And when I heard you talking to her, she didn't seem like the type of person who would help—"

"You're right," Bree said. "These are all bad ideas, so tell me you have something better."

The expression on Liz's face clearly indicated she didn't. And why would she? She was only a sixteen-year-old kid.

"We have to do something to *make* her come outside," Bree said. "We don't give her a choice. We provoke her somehow."

"A few months ago someone toilet-papered our trailer in the middle of the night. I was still awake, and it freaked me out because I didn't know what was happening, but I kept hearing noises. I woke up my dad, and when he realized what was happening, he ran outside and chased them off. Literally. He was *pissed*. They were on bicycles, and he took off down the street after them, screaming and cussing. I think it woke half the trailer park."

"Yeah… I don't think tee-peeing her house is going to have the desired effect."

"I didn't mean use toilet paper," Liz said, slightly defensively. "That was just an example. What if we went and got eggs? That would make her plenty mad. She'd come out for that."

"And then what?" Bree asked, unaware she was shooting holes in her own plan. "She comes outside, we run away, and we're no better off than where we started."

Liz bit her lip. "Unless it's only me who throws them. I get her to chase me, just like my dad chased those other kids, and when we're down the street, you go inside and get Tyler."

Bree opened her mouth to dispute the idea, then realized that could actually work... *if* Liz could make the woman angry enough to give chase. For that to happen, it had to be more than eggs. Eggs could be wiped clean. Liz needed to cause damage for this to work. Real damage. Bree thought back to Alissa spray-painting the word CHEATER on her gym teacher's car. Even though she had been furious at Alissa, she understood why Alissa had done it. Bree had her own incident of shame in high school: throwing a paving brick at the windshield of Patrick Gracey's new truck after learning he'd been cheating on Bree's best friend. It hadn't broken through the windshield as she thought it would (windshields, she learned later, were made from a special laminated glass), but it had damaged the glass beyond repair. Unlike Alissa, Bree hadn't been caught, and to this day, she still felt horrible about it. And now she was about to do it again, because house windows weren't made from a special laminated glass, and breaking one of those would definitely cause enough commotion (and rage) to drive someone out of their house.

"What are you thinking?" Liz asked.

Bree looked down at the tree in the yard next to them. Landscaping bricks circled the base, but it wasn't the bricks she was looking at, it was the rocks inside the circle. She went to the tree, dug out the biggest rock she could find, and shoved it into Liz's hand.

"You still want to help?" she asked Liz.

CHAPTER NINE

Bree knelt beside the fence in the neighbor's yard opposite the pimply boy's side, waiting for Liz to do what had to be done. Liz was a few feet away, hidden behind a tree, holding the rock in one hand… the same position she had been in for almost a full minute now. Liz was stalling and they both knew it. Bree had moved her truck two streets over to give Tyler's girlfriend the illusion she had left, and Liz had followed on her moped. Now, after walking back, they were doing a poor job of remaining inconspicuous. If it was a nicer neighborhood, one of the neighbors would have undoubtedly called the cops by now to report two suspicious characters.

"You got this," Bree told her in hushed voice. "All you have to do is run up to the house and throw the rock at the big picture window. Once it shatters, run back to the sidewalk to give yourself a good head start. As soon as the woman comes out, take off down the street. She'll follow you, but she won't catch you, and eventually she'll run out of steam and give up."

There was, of course, no way to know this for sure, but the woman was more than twice Liz's age and smoked, and Liz was fast on her feet. Both she and Alissa had played soccer up until sixth grade, and Liz had run circles around the entire team.

"Okay," Liz replied meekly.

Liz remained motionless, clearly terrified. She wasn't going to do it. It was too much to put on anyone, let alone a sixteen-year-old girl, and Bree knew it. So what did that leave? They didn't have time to stakeout the house for hours to wait and see if Tyler came out, so that meant it was back on Bree to do something. And the only thing Bree could think to do was break the window herself, stand her ground, and hope that Tyler truly was inside, would hear the crash, and come to investigate before the woman killed her. And if everything went right…

"Okay," Liz said again, and abruptly stepped out from behind the tree.

Bree's pulse shifted to a higher gear as she watched Liz approach the house, trip over a sinkhole, and lose her footing.

"Come on," Bree whispered as Liz scrambled back onto her feet. "Be fast—"

"Can I *help* you with something?"

It was the woman, Maggie, standing on her porch with her eyes on Liz, who looked like a small, trembling animal caught in a pair of headlights.

"Hey," Maggie barked, "girl on my lawn. Look at me."

Bree shrank back as Maggie padded across the yard and stopped a few feet short of Liz. The muscles in her jaw flexed when she saw the rock in Liz's hands.

"You want to explain why you're standing on my grass holding a stone the size of a golf ball?"

Liz had either forgotten how to speak or didn't know what to say. She swayed unsteadily on her feet, again looking over her shoulder.

"Well?" Maggie snapped. "You have something to say to me? Let me poke a blind stab at it: you're *also* here looking for Tyler Walker. Is that it? Or is it just a gigantic coincidence that you showed up fifteen minutes after that other girl who claimed to be Tyler's sister?"

Liz shook her head. "It's not a coincidence."

Maggie's eyes narrowed to the size of seeds as she tossed quick, jerky glances in all directions, her mouth an angry slit. "Where is she? Don't lie to me. I know when people are lying."

"I didn't want to do it," Liz said. Her voice was oddly calm, but Bree could see she was shaking. "She told me to throw a rock at your house and break your window, but I wasn't going to. I was only going to come to the door and beg you to talk to her. She's desperate to find her brother."

Maggie gave Liz an icy, measured stare. "You're telling me she really is Tyler's sister?"

"Yes."

"And their other sister really is in trouble? And if your 'friend' doesn't talk to Tyler, that sister might die?"

Liz was nodding ardently. "Everything she told you is true. You have to believe us, and you have to get Tyler."

Maggie looked far from convinced—that much was obvious even from a distance. Her hands remained fisted at her sides, and her eyebrows were drawn into a tight V. Liz wisely kept quiet, waiting for Maggie to process this information.

"Take me to her," Maggie said. "And don't insult me by saying she isn't nearby, waiting and hiding, because it's pretty obvious she is."

"Maybe you're right. And maybe I can go get her, and you can get Tyler, and we'll meet back here. Can we do that?"

Maggie smiled darkly. "You two must really think I'm stupid, don't you? Concocting this little skit in the hopes of getting me to bring Tyler outside when I haven't even admitted he's inside. Come to think of it, I'm not even sure that I *know* anyone named Tyler. So if you're done wasting my time—just like your friend did—I'm going to pretend this conversation never happened. And if you're not off this grass in thirty seconds, I'm going to see how far I can throw you."

"Okay," Liz said, inching backward toward the sidewalk, "I'll take you to Bree. You're right. She's hiding, and she's not far."

Bree steeled herself, ready to run—no, ready to fight. If this woman came at her, Bree was going to unleash everything she had. There was nowhere to run.

"Over here," Liz said, and all of Bree's breath came out in a rush as Liz began leading the woman in the opposite direction of where Bree was hiding.

"She's parked around the corner," Liz told the woman. "She's in her truck, waiting for me to come back. I was supposed to break your window and run away. She said that would teach you a lesson."

The two of them were across the street now, moving briskly. Bree was pitched forward, ready to break for the duplex as soon as they were out of sight. She guessed she had two, three minutes, tops. It would be enough. With that thought, she crept forward, her pulse thudding in her ears and temples as she trod quietly toward the front door. She was ten steps away. Eight. Liz and the woman were almost to the corner. Four steps. Three.

"What are you doing?" a voice boomed.

Bree jerked to a stop. The boy from next door was back at his window with his forehead pressed against the screen.

"Be quiet," Bree hissed. "Go away."

"Are you trying to steal from Maggie?" His voice climbed a register. "She's going to murder you if she catches you. Don't you see her? She's right across the street! Right now!"

Everything that came next happened fast.

There was an inarticulate sound of rage in the distance: Maggie, shrieking at Bree as she launched herself forward into a run. Liz shouting, telling Bree to get out of there. The boy chanting, "No, no, no!" as the dog unleashed a volley of barks from the backyard. And Bree herself, paralyzed as the woman closed the distance between them, still yelling, fists raised in the air.

"Go!" the boy cried, and Bree had no idea if he was talking about running away or going into the house. But there was no choice, because the woman was almost there, and before Bree realized what was happening, her feet pushed her forward, up the steps, into the house, where her hands somehow managed to stay steady long enough to slam and lock the front door behind her.

"Oh, shit," Bree whispered. "Shit, shit, shit."

The screen door flew open, and Bree recoiled as the woman pounded on the wooden door with both fists, rattling the frame. The horrific realization of what Bree had done sent a cramp of fear through her, and it took all her strength to keep her knees from buckling.

"Get out of my house!" the woman exploded. "Open this door!"

Bree could see her through the rectangular glass, her face red with fury. Bree backed away from the door, head whipping side to side. The living room was small, heavily populated with old furniture, and joined to a short hallway by dark-brown paneling.

"Tyler!" Bree shouted.

Bree lurched down the hallway, throwing open closed doors and tossing frantic glances into empty bedrooms and bathrooms. The fevered pounding on the front door came to an abrupt stop. Not good.

Bree stood at the edge of the hallway, bracing herself for whatever came next. When nothing happened, Bree crept forward, one hand gently touching the wall, and her breath came to a dead stop when she peered around the corner.

Maggie was gone.

"Shit," Bree whispered again.

The back door inside the kitchen exploded into an eruption of banging.

"I'm going to kill you!" Maggie hollered through the door, shaking the knob so violently Bree was sure it was going to fall off.

Bree's instinct was to escape through the front door, but there was another door that led into the basement—the only other place Tyler could be. Tyler had to be down there, and he wasn't answering because he was sleeping, or had on headphones, or was in the shower, or *something*. If Bree ran out of the duplex, she was no better off than she was before.

She hurried though the kitchen and took the stairs in a stumbling jog, barely putting one foot in front of the other, knowing that if Tyler wasn't there (and the woman got inside), Bree was probably going to die, and the police would probably side with the woman. Bree opened her mouth to yell Tyler's name, but the word died on her lips when she reached the bottom of the stairs.

The basement was a large, open room with Christmas lights strung across all four windowless walls. In the middle of the room was a long metal table filled with scales, baggies, ceramic bowls, and what looked to be lots and lots of green leaves. Some were loose in the bowls, some were rolled in the baggies, and it only took Bree a moment longer to realize two things simultaneously. The first was that the leaves were marijuana, and the second was that Tyler was nowhere in sight.

"Get out of my house!" Maggie shrieked from upstairs.

Bree's belief in God didn't extend past saying "bless you" when someone sneezed, but she rattled off a silent prayer as she opened the door across from her, hoping beyond hope that Tyler was inside, or that it at least led to an exit.

But it was only a bedroom with no bed. Toys were spread everywhere across the carpet, and dozens of old VHS movies were stacked knee-high under a shelf of games and puzzles.

"So not good," Bree said, glancing inside a tiny (and vacant) bathroom, before double-timing to her last option: accordion-style doors on the opposite wall. She knew it was only going to be a closet, but she still felt a nauseating drop in her stomach when she pulled open the doors and saw only hanging clothing. The woman hadn't been lying. Tyler wasn't there, and now Bree had no way out of the house except for up the stairs and out the front door.

The banging at the top of the stairs had ceased, and Bree didn't want to know what Maggie was going to do next. Bree needed to get out of the basement, but there were no windows—

There was a new sound: a thump and a tiny gasp. It had come from the closet.

"Hey," Bree said, raising her voice but keeping her distance. "Is someone in there?" And then in a stronger voice: "Tyler?"

One of the coats moved. Bree was about to call out again when a child, surely no more than five or six, stepped out between a long, red dress and an old leather trench coat. The girl was wearing a puffy, blue princess dress that looked like an old Halloween costume, and there were temporary tattoos of faded hearts on both of her cheeks. Her eyes stayed on Bree as she clutched the sleeve of a furry winter coat, as if letting go might cause her to sink into the carpet.

"Who are you?" Bree choked.

"Are you here to take me away?" the girl asked. "Are you one of the"—she lowered her chin and voice—"*bad* people?"

Bree blinked at the girl's words, trying to reconcile this new development. A little girl, hiding in the basement closet inside a room filled with drugs. There was no way things could get any more messed up.

"No," Bree said finally, trying to think of something else to say, and mostly coming up blank. "I would never try and take a little girl away from her mommy."

The girl considered this as she lifted her head toward Maggie's shouts and pounding. "Then why is Mommy so mad?"

"She's not mad," Bree said after a beat. "She's frustrated, because she's trying to do something in the backyard and it's not working. But she knows I'm down here."

"So... you're a friend of my mommy?"

"I'm a friend of a *friend* of your mommy. And I'm here looking for him. His name is Tyler."

A broad smile filled the girl's face. "Tyler's my friend, too!"

"You know Tyler?"

Before the girl could answer, there was a splintering crash of wood upstairs—Maggie kicking open the back door. She was inside the duplex.

"I don't like that sound," the girl said, backing away with a whimper. "That's a scary sound."

Fear swept over Bree as she frantically glanced around, knowing there was no place to escape. Footsteps erupted on the staircase, and Bree shrank back as Maggie launched down the remaining basement steps, but instead of going for Bree, she scooped up the girl and held her fiercely in her arms.

"Are you okay?" Maggie rasped.

"Don't be mad at me, Mommy," the girl said and burst into tears.

Bree started to speak, to say she was sorry—to say anything to convey how horrible she felt—but the words caught in her throat when another figure appeared halfway down the steps, gaping at her.

"What the hell, Bree?" Tyler croaked.

All Bree's energy drained from her legs as she looked at her brother, unsure if she wanted to hug him or strangle him.

CHAPTER TEN

Bree sat rigid at Maggie's kitchen table with her hands in her lap. Tyler and Maggie were having a heated discussion at the end of the hallway, and it took everything inside Bree to stay seated and calm, waiting for Tyler to smooth things over. Liz had texted multiple times from outside to find out what was happening, and Bree had told her to wait and stay put. Hopefully Liz would. Bree's eyes skipped to the clock above the sink—almost nine—then to the broken back door that Tyler had kicked open to get inside. If Maggie had simply said Tyler was at the store and would be home soon, all of this could have been avoided.

The talking from the hallway abruptly stopped. Bree stiffened as Maggie came into the kitchen and took a seat at the table, followed by Tyler, who lingered inside the living room with his arms crossed. Whatever Tyler had said to Maggie must have worked… but just barely. Maggie's hands were clasped into a tight ball on top of the table, and there was pure murder in her eyes.

"Mommy?" It was the little girl, her voice drifting out from the hallway. "Can I come out of my room now? I'm thirsty."

"Come on out," Maggie said flatly. "You can have some juice."

"I got it," Tyler said. He went to the fridge, pulled out a glass jug of orange juice, and began filling a plastic cup from the counter. The girl appeared at the edge of the hallway, peering into the kitchen at Bree.

"Go back into your room, baby," Maggie said. "The grown-ups have to talk."

The girl frowned. "But you always say juice stays in the kitchen. Because of spills."

"It's okay. This one time." Her eyes stayed on Bree as she spoke. "Go on, now. And try real, real hard not to spill. Okay? But if you do, I won't be mad. Not this time."

The girl padded off out of the kitchen. As soon as she was gone, Tyler seemed to deflate, running a hand across his mouth and shaking his head.

"I'm sorry for this, Maggie," Tyler said. "I never—"

"You don't get to talk anymore," Maggie said.

Tyler flinched. "What?"

"You've known me long enough to know how I operate. No drama. I went against my better judgment to let you stay here, but I did, and that's on me. But *this*"—she waved an angry hand in Bree's direction—"is the final straw. Your sister tricked her way into my house. *Locked* me outside. I was two seconds away from breaking a window and breaking every bone in your sister's body. And what would have happened to Josie if I'd done that? You tell me what would have happened."

"Maggie," Tyler began, "it's not—"

"Go pack your shit," she told him. "I'm going to have a few words with your sister, and then I want you gone."

Tyler glared at Bree, started to speak, but instead threw up his hands and disappeared down the hallway.

"We're going to keep this real simple," Maggie said to Bree. "I'm going to talk, and you're going to keep quiet and listen to me, word for word, without interrupting. Can you do that?"

Bree started to answer, and then decided it was better to simply nod.

"Good. Now, the way I see it, you broke into my house, which is a crime. To make matters even worse for you, my daughter was inside the house, and for all I know, it was your intention to kidnap her. Or hurt her."

Maggie leaned forward, daring Bree to speak. It took all of Bree's resolve to stay quiet. Bree nodded again, once.

"Those are charges that I know the cops would take very, very seriously. I'm sure you agree. The reason I'm *not* going to call the cops is because you, in all your bold stupidness, stumbled across my business venture in the basement. I'm not going to sugarcoat it: I sell weed to blue-collar workers in the surrounding neighborhoods who want to unwind and relax. I'm small time. I do it because I have a shit job at a shit clothing store that pays a shit wage, and I have a daughter to take care of who doesn't have a daddy in the picture—and yes, I realize that if I got caught, my daughter would be taken away from me… but if I can't afford to put a roof over my daughter's head, or food in my daughter's mouth, then I'm no good to her anyway. So it's a necessary evil. Sometimes we have to do what we have to do."

"Yes," Bree said. "I know that."

Maggie nodded once. "Maybe you do, and maybe you don't. But that doesn't change the facts or the quandary we've stepped into. Or maybe there is no quandary. Maybe you didn't break into my house; and maybe you didn't see anything in my basement; and maybe it would be best if everyone just went their separate ways and left it at that. I'm guessing that's an option you could live with?"

"I could."

"Tyler!" Maggie hollered, wasting no time. "We're done!"

Tyler appeared at the edge of the hallway, making Bree wonder if he had been there the entire time. He probably had.

"Are you packed?" Maggie asked.

"Maggie, come on."

Maggie stood from the table. "Get packed and get out. Both of you."

Tyler shot an angry glance at Bree before disappearing back into the hallway. Bree quickly followed and found him in the farthest bedroom throwing a duffle bag onto the bed.

"I had a good thing going here," he said, opening a dresser drawer.

"A good thing? Your girlfriend is crazy. The basement is full of illegal drugs, and there's a little girl living here who's terrified the cops are going to come and take her mother away to prison. How is any of this a good thing, Tyler?"

"I didn't ask you to come here," Tyler said. "I didn't ask to be found—"

"Someone took Alissa," Bree said in a voice that wasn't steady, "and said the only way to get her back is to give them you."

Tyler had stopped packing and was staring at Bree in disbelief. "What?"

"What did you do?" Bree choked.

"I didn't do anything."

Something inside Bree broke, and the tears came hard and fast, coursing down her cheeks as she stumbled backward into the wall and slid to the floor. Tyler raised his hands, looking like a helpless, lost child, unsure what to do next.

"What did you *do*?" Bree said again in a voice that was barely a whisper.

CHAPTER ELEVEN

By the time Bree finished explaining everything, her mouth had gone dry, and Tyler looked as if he had aged ten years. He sat on the edge of the bed, staring into the photograph of Alissa.

"If you're done packing," Maggie said, appearing at the bedroom door, "then go."

Tyler lifted his head like a man drugged. For a moment he only gaped at Maggie, as if he wasn't sure where he was or what was happening, before rising and slinging the duffel bag over his shoulder. He looked as if he wanted to say something, but he only stared at his feet as he left the room. Bree silently followed as Maggie trailed them to the front door.

"Are you going away?"

It was the little girl, standing in the kitchen with a deep frown.

"Josie," Maggie said sharply. "I told you to stay in your bedroom."

"I have to go," Tyler said, squatting to Josie's eye level. "I have to help my sister with something, but I'll be back before you know it."

"Like tomorrow? You said you were going to help me make a fort from the couch pillows today, but we never did, so I was going to wake up early tomorrow so we could do it then."

Tyler tried to smile. "We are totally making a pillow fort. Probably not tomorrow, but we will soon."

"Do you have to go? I don't want you to, not even for one bedtime." She leaned into him and whispered, "I like you the most of my mommy's friends."

"You better," he told her. "Promise me you won't use your boogers as glue when making construction paper animals when I'm gone."

Josie's eyes widened. "You know about that?"

"I know *everything*," Tyler said, drawing out the word. He lowered his gaze at her. "I also know you drew a flower inside the bathroom closet, but I know you'll be a good girl and erase it before your mom finds it."

Josie gave a sullen nod. "Okay."

"Give me one for the road."

Maggie stiffened as Josie gave Tyler a hug.

"We should go," Bree said, eyeing Maggie, who was clearly unmoved by the exchange. "Tyler."

Tyler tousled Josie's hair. "Stay cool, fool."

"I will, anthill." Josie giggled, sending a wave of déjà vu through Bree. It was something Bree had always said to Alissa growing up, and it caught her off guard to hear it come from Tyler's mouth. The entire display had caught her off guard. Tyler had always been paternal toward Alissa, but to see him this way with someone else's child was bizarre, especially under the circumstances.

"I'm sorry," Tyler said, giving Maggie a sideways glance. "I'll call you when this is all sorted."

Maggie said nothing. The moment Bree and Tyler were outside, the door slammed and locked behind them. Tyler jerked back in surprise when Liz appeared from behind the trees.

"What's she doing here?" he asked Bree.

Bree gave a grunt of disgust. "After everything I just told you, *that's* what you're concerned about? You need to start talking and tell me what's going on."

"I don't know what you want me to say."

"I want you to come clean about what you did that caused this."

"And I'm telling you," he answered crossly, "that I haven't done anything."

"Haven't done anything," Bree echoed dryly. "Just like that time you didn't go joyriding on that stolen—I mean, *borrowed*—dirt bike before crashing it into that bus stop shelter. Or that time you didn't set fire to that dumpster in the alley behind that Chinese restaurant." She shook her head. "There aren't enough hours in the day to name all the questionable things you've done, Tyler, and it scares the hell out of me to think about all the things that I *don't* know you've done. So don't stand there and try and play innocent."

Maggie's porch light flicked off, on, and back off.

"We can't stay here," Tyler said. "Where's your truck?"

"It's two streets over," Liz chimed in, pointing down the street. "That way. With my moped."

Tyler took off with Liz in tow. The porch light snapped back on, and Bree saw Maggie staring at her through the window, head lowered, arms crossed. Bree didn't need to be warned again. She trailed after Tyler and Liz, catching a snippet of hushed conversation that stopped as soon as Bree caught up.

"So you can share secrets with Liz but not me?" Bree asked.

Tyler gave Bree a steely glare over his shoulder. "I told her she shouldn't be here. Why in God's name would you bring her along?"

It was on the tip of Bree's tongue to tell him what Alissa had tried to do with their mother's pills, but now wasn't the time or place.

"And to answer your question from earlier," Tyler added, "I haven't jacked any cars lately, robbed any banks, or killed any hookers. Okay?"

Bree drew a sharp breath. "There has to be something you know that you're not telling me."

"There isn't."

"Then it's something you're overlooking. Whoever has Alissa is someone who knows you. Have you made any enemies lately? Anyone who wants to hurt you?"

"No."

"Not one person?" Bree pressed. "You're telling me you can't think of *one* single person that you've wronged. Someone who might want to cause you harm."

"I don't know," Tyler said, shifting his duffel bag from one hand to the other. "I'm sure there's people in this world that don't like me, but no one that's out to get me. Even you've rubbed people the wrong way, Bree. It happens to everybody."

Bree's truck was just ahead. "Don't just gloss over this, Tyler. You need to think, and think carefully. Anyone. For any reason."

"How many times do you want me to tell you the same thing? I don't know. Can you give me two seconds to think or breathe?" He pulled ahead of her, tossed his bag into the bed of the truck, and out of nowhere slammed his fist into the passenger door, eliciting a cry of pain and rage.

"Calm down," Liz said.

Tyler whirled on her. "Some lunatic has Alissa and the only way she'll be safe is if I take her place, and you want me to calm down?"

He stormed away from the truck. When Liz started after him, Bree stopped her with a hand. "Leave him be."

"I was only trying to help," Liz said in a small voice.

Tyler had only gone as far as the corner street lamp and Bree approached him cautiously.

"What am I supposed to do," Tyler said heavily. "Go to them? Give myself up?"

Bree's heart skipped a beat. This was the moment she'd been dreading, because Liz had been right: they couldn't just let Tyler go. They couldn't just trade one sibling for another.

"No," she said firmly. "What we do now is think. We figure out why this is happening and who's doing it. And to do that, you need to retrace your life these last few days. Or weeks. Maybe even months."

"Months," he said. "I can barely remember what I did this morning after I woke up at Maggie's."

"Then we start with Maggie. Do you help her sell the drugs?"

"It's not *drug* drugs, like cocaine or meth; it's just pot. It's harmless."

"Whatever," Bree said. "I'm not interested in a political debate on the harmful effects of drugs. The simple fact is that weed is illegal and she's selling it. Are you helping her?"

"Maybe," he mumbled.

Bree shook her head. "Maybe? So *yes*?"

"Sometimes," he replied irritably. "Maggie never sells it at her house. She always meets people. Sometimes, if she's not sure about them, I go with her. You know… hang in the background, act tough. The muscle."

"Are you selling a bad product? Maybe a bad batch? Did you move into another drug lord's territory, and now they want revenge? Is there a rival gang also competing for the business?"

"Christ, Bree, you watch too many movies. It's not like that. She mostly sells to college kids or working stiffs who like to get high on the weekends and chill."

"Then what about Maggie? How long have you been together? How did you meet?"

Tyler sighed. "I've known Maggie for a few years. She was my supervisor when I worked at Bonebrake Video."

"Worked" was one way to put it. Bonebrake Video had been a dying, hole-in-the-wall nook where very few people came to rent DVDs. Mostly it was a hangout for the local potheads and stoners who wanted to talk movies and their dreams of making one. Tyler's part-time employment there had run its course in two months. It had since closed and was now an equally dingy used video game store, where Bree imagined the same potheads and stoners came to hang out.

"Maggie and I bumped into each other last month and started hanging out again. It was nothing romantic at first; that part just kinda happened. And it was nothing serious, just casual."

"What about the little girl's father?" Bree asked. "Is he in the picture at all? Did she kick him out? Is he jealous? Any chance he's involved because you're with Maggie?"

"Do you know how dumb that sounds? Why would he kidnap Alissa over that? If he felt raw about me being with his ex-girlfriend, don't you think he'd just come at me, especially since I've been staying with Maggie?"

Bree bolstered her patience. "You know, it's real easy to sit there and shoot down everything I say, so how about you offer up some ideas? I'm just trying to think of anything, okay? If you don't think it has anything to do with the drugs or Maggie, what else is there? Do you owe someone money?"

"Maybe a few people," Tyler said. "I've borrowed money from friends over the years that probably never got paid back. Nothing that would make someone come after our family."

"Where were you staying before you met up with Maggie?"

"Just around," Tyler answered with a shrug. "Before Maggie's, I was crashing on an old buddy's couch."

"Which buddy?"

"Vince. You don't know him. He's an old friend."

"Did you guys get into trouble together? Steal something?"

"No," Tyler said impatiently. "Why would you think I stole something?"

"Someone abducted our sister because of something you did, Tyler, which means that person is either insane or something extreme drove them to do it. I keep asking myself what that thing could be, and my mind keeps coming back to money. Almost everything shitty in this world comes back to money."

"So that's what you think of me. That I'm a thief."

"I don't know what to think. It's been almost a month since I last saw you. Up until an hour ago, I didn't know you had a girlfriend, or that you were basically homeless. I'm afraid to ask how you support yourself. I'm guessing you don't have a job. So if it's not money this person is after, then you tell me what else it could be—"

"Dave," Tyler said abruptly.

Bree drew back. "What?"

"Our Uncle Dave," Tyler stammered, almost shouting it. His hands moved left and right, making circles, as if pulling the information from the air. "I mean, not *him*, but you asked me earlier if I had any enemies. If there was a reason that someone might be after me…"

His words lingered as Bree waited for her brother to continue. Tyler's head was lowered in thought, his eyes open but faraway.

"A couple of weekends ago, I ran into Dave at the liquor store… and before you say anything, I know you don't want anything to do with Dave anymore, but what happened between him and Mom is between them, so save your lecture, okay?"

"Whatever," Bree said briefly. "Just tell me."

"Dave said he had a buddy visiting, and they were looking to score something to blow off some steam. I think he had hoped for something stronger than weed, but beggars can't be choosers, and I told him I'd come by his house later that night. Maggie wasn't thrilled when I told her because she didn't know either of them, but Dave had always been a straight shooter with me, and if he was vouching for his buddy, I figured he was legit. Plus, I knew Maggie needed the money. She insisted on coming with me, so we left Josie with a friend and headed over. I figured five minutes in and out and all would be good. No big deal. But it turned into a big deal… and some shit kind of went down."

"What kind of shit?"

Tyler was shaking his head. "I can't believe I didn't put this together when you first asked me, but I was so caught off guard—"

"Tyler," Bree said peevishly, "what *kind* of shit? And what does any of this have to do with Alissa?"

"So, Maggie and I go to Dave's house, and this guy, Dave's buddy, totally reminds me of Mom's cousin Ted. Remember him? When he sometimes visited in the summers when we were kids?"

Bree did. Ted was a small guy with an unruly beard and long, stringy hair who always dressed in flannel shirts and rarely bathed. He hadn't been a man of many words (Bree had always guessed it was because half his teeth were rotten and the other half were missing—a walking advertisement for the perils of skipping the dentist, their mother always warned), and when Ted did speak, what came out had been more of a fumbling stutter than a functioning sentence.

"Dave's buddy looked just like Ted," Tyler said, "but he wasn't anywhere near as mellow as Ted. No, this guy had a hard look in his eyes, and he talked in rapid bursts using his hands, and was super high-strung. I've known tons of guys like that in my life, and they're always trouble. They always have a chip on their shoulder, and they're quick to fly off the handle over any little thing. Even worse, it was clear he and Dave had been drinking. But everything went fine, we did the deal, and went to leave. But when we got outside, Emma was there."

"Who?"

Tyler took a breath. "Before I reconnected with Maggie, I'd been dating this girl named Emma for a few weeks. She was nice, but she was young, and she got clingy really fast. She was also a little… *off*, is the only way to describe it. She had this quiet intensity about her, but sometimes she'd just burst out laughing at totally inappropriate things. I never knew what she was thinking."

Tyler looked like he wanted to add more, but didn't seem to know what, or how.

"I'd been blowing Emma off for a few days," Tyler went on, "hoping she'd get the hint, but she kept texting me, and I kept making excuses that I was busy, or I'd just ignore the texts. And yes… I know it was an asshole move, but let's just skip the speech, okay?"

"I don't care about any of that. Why was that girl Emma there?"

"She *followed* me. In the short time we dated, we never went to her place—we always hung out at Vince's apartment. So while I never knew where she lived, she knew exactly where to find me. And since I'd been blowing her off, she apparently took it upon herself to wait outside Vince's and watch for me. When Maggie picked me up, Emma followed us to Dave's house. That's messed up, right?"

Tyler paused, as if waiting for some sort of acknowledgement, and Bree gave him an impatient nod to continue.

"It was bad, Bree. Emma was freaking out and sobbing and screaming at me. Telling me how horrible I was. How I had mistreated her. Asking how I could do this to her. The way she was going on, you'd have thought I'd murdered someone in her family. I didn't know what to do. I mean, I've had some ugly breakups before—some of them in public—and I can handle that… but this wasn't a good time or place to be drawing attention to ourselves. There was a good chunk of weed inside Dave's house, and Maggie had a good chunk of cash crammed into her pockets. Dave wasn't happy, and his friend started getting really agitated."

Tyler ran a hand across his mouth. Perspiration had gathered on his forehead. Liz had crept away from the truck and was trying to listen, but Tyler paid no notice.

"Maggie had already retreated to the car," he went on, "and I was left there trying to talk Emma down and also explain to Dave that this hysterical girl had nothing to do with our business and everything was fine. But Dave's buddy wasn't having it. He was getting more pissed every passing second, and then…" Tyler shook his head as he met Bree's eyes. "Then I realized that Dave's friend wasn't pissed at me because Emma was making a scene and drawing attention to us… he was pissed because I was cheating on Emma. He was siding with Emma *against* me, telling me that's no way to treat a lady, and I was a piece of shit for doing what I was doing. Do you believe that? I don't even know this guy, and he was defending this girl and getting in my face."

Tyler's expression turned hard.

"And then he swung at me." Tyler whacked his right cheek. "Hit me straight on, right there. I didn't even see it coming. And if it wasn't for the fact that this guy was nothing more than a beanpole or that I knew how to take a punch, he might have hurt me. Maybe even knocked me down. But neither of those things happened, and once I regained my balance, I saw red and lit into him. One second the guy was standing in front of me, the next second he was sprawled out across the pavement. That was when I saw the blood."

"Blood?" Liz asked.

Tyler looked like he wanted to crawl out of his skin as he relived the memory. "The guy's head was laid out across the concrete steps. I don't know if the blood was from where I hit him in his mouth or because he cracked open his skull, but there was a lot of it. He wasn't moving."

"Jesus, Tyler," Bree said.

"Maggie had the car running with the passenger door open and was shouting for me to *come on...* so I did. I turned tail and ran. What else could I do?"

"That's why you disappeared," Bree said as everything fell into place. "That's why you stopped coming around the trailer and we hadn't seen you."

Tyler's face soured. "I didn't know what was going to happen next, but I knew I couldn't stay at Vince's anymore. Dave didn't know I was staying there, but Emma did. What if I seriously hurt that guy and the police got involved and came looking for me? Or what if the police found the drugs and Dave told them they were from me?" Tyler released a controlled breath. "I went straight to Vince's, grabbed my shit, and started staying with Maggie. I didn't leave her house for days, mostly hiding in the basement, waiting for the cops to show up at the front door. But they never did, because no one knew I was there. I eventually convinced myself that Dave's friend was okay, and that Dave hadn't sold me out, and went on with my life."

"And you don't know what happened to the guy?"

Tyler shook his head. "No. And it's not like I was going to call up Dave and ask. About a week ago, I talked to Dad to see if anyone had been asking about me, and Dad said no, but now it's pretty clear."

"What is?"

"That *guy*," Tyler said. "You asked if I could think of any reason that someone might be after me. Dave's buddy isn't the type of guy who's just going to forget the beat-down I gave him. He's going to want revenge. Hell, I would if I were him. He came looking for me, found Alissa, and took her to draw me out."

"You really think that guy might have something to do with Alissa?" Liz asked, not trying to hide the fact that she had listened to the entire conversation.

"I don't know," Tyler said, starting for the truck, "but I think we need to pay Dave a visit."

Bree's heart picked up speed as she followed. "We just go there and casually ask him if his buddy has abducted our sister?"

"You asked me if I had any idea who might be doing this. This is *something*. It can't be a coincidence. If you don't want to go with me, I'll go alone. But I'm going to talk to Dave."

Bree could tell by the look on his face he meant it. And it wasn't like she could stop him. Not when he was like this. It was one of the few traits she shared with her brother: once something was put into his mind, it was nearly impossible to change it.

"Are we going?" Liz asked.

"Okay," Bree said. "We go see Dave."

Bree started for the driver's side and abruptly stopped when Liz began to follow.

"What?" Liz asked. "What's wrong?"

"You're not coming."

Liz flinched so violently, a passerby might have thought she'd been slapped by an invisible hand. "What do you mean I'm not coming?"

"I get that you still want to help, and you have. A lot. If not for you, the situation at the duplex could have been way worse. But as far as what Tyler and I are going to do now… I don't know how things are going to play out."

"I don't care—"

"But I do," Bree said with mounting irritation. She was tired of arguing and justifying her every decision with a sixteen-year-old that wasn't Alissa. "I shouldn't have brought you this far, but I did. But now it's over. You're done. Go home and stay safe."

Bree circled around the truck and climbed inside. The moment she put the key in the ignition, she heard the moped sputter to life, and saw Liz staring back at her in the rearview mirror.

"She's going to follow us there," Bree said.

"Who cares?" Tyler said. "Just go. We can't stop her."

Bree gave Liz a final, frustrated glance before dropping the truck into gear. "If anything happens to her, that's also on you."

She stomped on the gas, knowing it was a shit thing to say, but also knowing it was the truth. All of this was on Tyler.

And if they survived, Bree was going to kill him.

CHAPTER TWELVE

"You're sure this is it?" Bree asked again.

"Yes," Tyler answered again. "I told you I was here. I remember."

Bree nodded, more to herself than Tyler. It wasn't so much that she thought Tyler couldn't remember; it was more that she had never been here before, and she couldn't believe their uncle lived in a place this sketchy. The house was an old two-story set back from the road, and while the blue paint appeared to be from this decade, the siding was warped and cracked (and flat out missing) in various places. Most of the roof shingles were crumbling. One of the second-floor windows was covered with plywood. The driveway was empty, and with the exception of a single light inside the kitchen, the rest of the house was dark. It had been almost ten minutes since they had parked across the street, hidden in the shadow of a massive oak tree, and in that time, there had been no movement from inside. Dave was either gone, asleep, or passed out.

"Do we just sit and wait for something to happen?" Bree asked.

"I don't know. I'm thinking."

Bree settled back into her seat and checked the rearview mirror. Liz was parked behind the truck, still on her moped, arms crossed.

"How did you find me, anyway?" Tyler asked.

"Dad," Bree answered reluctantly.

Tyler drew back in the seat, studying her as if she might be putting him on. The look on his face suggested he had something to say (or *lots* to say), but if so, he was keeping it to himself.

"I didn't have much choice," Bree said evenly. "The last phone number I had for you was disconnected, and you haven't been by the trailer in forever. I knew if anyone knew where you were, it would be him."

"I'm sorry."

Bree wasn't sure if Tyler was apologizing for the disconnected number or that he had forced her to go see their father, but it really made no difference: Tyler lived in a perpetual state of sorryness, and everyone in the family, Tyler included, knew that would probably never change.

Tyler shifted in his seat. "Was that…" He glanced in the side mirror at Liz, even though there was no way she was close enough to hear. "Was that the first time you'd seen him since—"

"Yes," Bree answered curtly.

A silence fell between them. Tyler knew better than to say anything more. There was nothing more *to* say. No reason to relive that night… even though it was already unfolding inside Bree's head, just as it had a hundred times already during the last six months. Their mother washing dishes at the kitchen sink. Alissa doing homework at the kitchen table instead of her bedroom, because she had been grounded for ditching math class the week before, and that meant homework was done "out in the open" where she wouldn't be distracted by her phone or television. Bree folding laundry by the couch, enjoying the tranquility of the evening… until she heard the screech of tires on the pavement out front… the slamming of a car door… their father's heavy footsteps on the porch. But it wasn't their father—it was their father's younger brother, Dave, who lived across town and rarely visited. He didn't knock or say anything, only stormed into the trailer and made straight for Bree's mother…

"David?" Cassie asked, surprised. "What are you doing here?"

Dave's face was sheet-white. "I'm sorry for barging in like this. I didn't know what else to do."

"Do about what?" she asked. "Is it Beth? Is she okay?"

The question seemed to derail him. His lips moved, but nothing came out. Alissa had risen from the table and moved closer to Bree. The last time they had seen Dave was at his and Beth's wedding a few years back, which had ended with Dave and their father getting so drunk the hotel had shut down the reception early. Dave, like their father, was a violent drunk, and God help anyone who stood between him and his liquor.

"Jack knows," Dave finally said emphatically, as if that explained everything. "I told Beth the truth, and she was so upset she locked herself in the bathroom. I tried to get her to come out, but she wouldn't listen… and then I heard her talking to someone. When she eventually came out she said she had left a message on Jack's cell phone and told him everything."

All the color left Cassie's cheeks.

"I thought it would be okay," Dave said. "It's been over seventeen years now. I thought enough time had passed. I thought… I thought Beth would understand and forgive—"

"Why?" Cassie asked. Her hands were trembling and Bree didn't know if it was from anger or fear. "Why would you do this? Why now?"

His mouth twitched at the corners. "I'm sober. I mean… I'm trying. I'm going through the program. Step six or seven or one of those says we need to make amends with people we've wronged, and I knew I could never tell Jack, but Beth…" He let out a shuddering breath. "She's my wife, for God's sake. I thought I could trust her to deal with it. I knew she'd be mad, but I never expected… I never…"

"Mom?" Bree asked, finding her voice. "What's he talking about?"

"I'm sorry," Dave said. His feet were pedaling him back toward the door. "You need to get out of here before Jack gets off work and listens to that message. Go somewhere else. Just don't be here."

The screen door opened and closed. Bree went to the window and watched Dave scurry back toward his car.

"I tried, you know."

Bree lifted her head. She was back in her truck, hands gripping the bottom of the steering wheel, cold sweat beading on her forehead.

"I tried," Tyler said again. There was a noticeable shift in his tone. "Over the next few weeks, after everything had calmed down, I visited Dad. More than once. Talked to him. Tried to smooth things over."

"And we all know how well that went," Bree said, and swung to face her brother. "And that's the worst part. Maybe—*maybe*—I could move past what he did that night at the trailer. I know Dad well enough to know how out of control he gets when he's drunk and pissed. I get that. That's something we've all learned to live with over the years. But for him to still refuse to see Alissa and throw away their relationship like it means nothing?" Bree shook her head. "That I can't move past, because Alissa still wants him in her life. She wants a father, even if it's only him."

Tyler's lips were pressed tightly together, and Bree knew he was gauging what to say (or not say) next. The subject of their father had always been the biggest point of contention in their relationship. She could never understand how Tyler could have any respect for the man. Tyler hadn't been there that night, but he had been there too many other nights to count, always defending their father to the police—their father was drunk; their father didn't mean it; their father had just had a bad day—even though the end result was usually the same: Jack Walker getting dragged off in handcuffs.

"So yeah," Bree said, "to answer your original question, I went and saw Dad, and it sucked. Thanks so much for that."

Tyler was quiet for a minute. "Did he tell you about Alcoholics Anonymous?"

Bree gave a cryptic laugh. "Yeah. Right before he got angry at something I said and looked like he wanted to throw me against the wall, just like the old days."

"He's trying, Bree. That's all he can do."

"Like you, Tyler?"

His face knotted. "What does that mean?"

"We're here because you lost your temper and seriously injured a guy over a girlfriend you decided to blow off. And by 'girlfriend,' I mean the girl you were messing around with before you hooked up with a woman twice your age—"

"That's enough," Tyler said. His eyes blazed at Bree. "I'm not going to sit here and defend every shitty thing I've ever done in my life. And yeah, *Bree*, I've done a lot of things I'm not proud of. But that doesn't mean I don't try to be better. Not everyone in the world has your incredible self-control and motivation; did you ever think about that? Did you ever stop to think that the reason I don't hate Dad is because I know how easy it is to be a screw-up? To do and say stupid things in the heat of the moment, only to regret them later?" Tyler's voice warbled. "I know I'm like Dad. I *know* that. But if I give up on Dad and don't believe that he has the ability to change for the better… then what chance is there for me?"

The rock in Bree's stomach shifted. Tyler turned away, shaking his head. A hundred things sprang to Bree's lips, but she found herself afraid to speak for fear of saying the wrong thing. Because deep down, she knew she often sold Tyler short. Was quick to call him out on everything (she believed) he did wrong. But there was more to Tyler than most people knew. He was fiercely loyal to his family. Always had the patience and time to listen to Alissa's problems, no matter how petty they seemed to Bree. And inasmuch as Tyler always defended their father, Tyler was also quick to put himself in harm's way to protect whoever was on the receiving end of his father's wrath.

"Tyler," Bree said, "I—"

"There," Tyler said, pointing across the street. Their uncle had emerged from the house and was dragging a small garbage bag to the curb. His hair was a mess as if he had just rolled out of bed, and he was wearing a ratty T-shirt and shorts. He left the bag, glanced around, and started back toward the house.

"Now what?" Bree asked.

Tyler either didn't hear or didn't feel the need to answer; he was already out of the truck and marching across the street with purpose.

"Dave!" Tyler called out as Dave reached the door. Dave's eyes went wide as he turned and saw Tyler, and he clawed open the screen door like he had just spotted the devil.

"*Shit!*" Bree exclaimed, fumbling with her door handle.

"What's happening?" Liz asked.

"Stay there," Bree snapped. Bree broke into a run as Tyler followed Dave into the house. When she reached the door, Dave and Tyler were squared off inside the kitchen—Tyler with both hands raised, and Dave gripping an aluminum baseball bat.

"Whoa," Bree said, slowly stepping inside. "Everyone take it easy."

Tyler's head turned briefly in Bree's direction, but his eyes stayed on Dave. "Are you going to hit me with that, Dave? You really want to do this?"

"I oughta break your skull," Dave said.

Tyler pulled a switchblade from his pocket and snapped it open. "Try it."

"Tyler," Bree shrilled, "put that away—"

"He knows something, Bree," Tyler said leaning sideways, trying to see past Dave into the dark living room. "Is your buddy hiding in there? Hey! You in there?"

Dave tightened his grip on the bat. "You think Joel is here after what you did? He's in jail."

"Jail?" Bree asked. "The guy Tyler hurt is in jail? Are you sure?"

Dave's face darkened. "Am I *sure*? Do you have any idea what your brother did that night?"

"Tell me," she said. "I've heard Tyler's side of the story, so tell me yours."

For a moment she didn't think Dave was going to answer. The vein on his forehead bulged as drew in a ragged breath, and after another beat, he lowered the bat, but only slightly.

"Joel's a hothead," Dave said. "He started the shit with Tyler, and that was dumb. After Tyler knocked him out, I didn't know what to do, and before I could figure it out, Tyler was driving off and leaving me with his mess."

Tyler gave Bree a sideways glance. "I told you, I panicked—"

"Joel came around pretty fast," Dave went on. "He had a bad cut on his head that was bleeding, but otherwise he seemed okay. Groggy and pissed off, but okay. I was helping him to his feet when the police cruiser rolled up. One of the neighbors had called and reported the disturbance."

"Are you saying Joel went to jail because they found the weed?" Tyler asked angrily. "I hope to hell you didn't give them my name—"

"I didn't have a chance. As soon as Joel saw the officers, he tried to run. He didn't get very far in his condition, and when one of the officers tackled him, a goddamn revolver fell out of the back of his pants."

The air left Bree's lungs. "He had a gun?"

"Did you know about that?" Tyler asked.

"Hell no," Dave said, looking back and forth between them. "I also didn't know he had a warrant out for his arrest. First degree robbery in Leichty County, which would explain why he was so insistent on coming to visit and stay with me. Apparently, Joel's idea of lying low is to put his friends at risk."

This time it was Bree's turn to give Tyler a sideways glance.

"So to answer your question again," Dave said sourly to Bree, "yeah… I'm sure Joel's in jail. He isn't going to make bail, and the last I heard, he's still waiting for the preliminary hearing. And if the cops had come into the house and found the weed, I'd be in there with him." Dave gave a tsk of disgust. "You screwed up a lot of lives that night. I'm not saying Joel was a saint, but he was my friend, and you put me in a horrible position. Not to mention what happened to that girl who followed you here."

Tyler straightened. "Emma? What about her?"

"You don't know? That figures. As soon as you drove off, she got in her SUV and raced out of here. I don't know if she was trying to chase you down or just get away from here, but it didn't work."

"What didn't work?" Bree asked carefully.

Dave's brow furrowed. "After Joel was hauled away, I got it in my head to drive to the police station to see if I could do anything to help. I mean, you're my nephew, and it was my idea to have you come over, so I felt like I was the one who caused this. I didn't know exactly what I expected to do, or even if they'd let me see Joel, but I was going stir crazy just sitting there. When I turned at the end of my street, I saw a tow truck operator hooking up an SUV that had crashed into a tree. The front end was totaled, and when I drove past, I realized it was the SUV that girl had been driving."

Bree looked at Tyler, who was staring at their uncle in disbelief. "Emma's SUV? Are you sure?"

"The girl wasn't there," Dave said, "but I recognized the SUV right away—not just because of the color and make, but also because of the rear window decal of the cartoon dog with a heart. It was hers. She obviously crashed it after she left here."

"Jesus," Bree said. "Did the crash look bad? Do you think Emma was hurt?"

"I don't know. Like I said, the front end was totaled, and I could see that the airbags had deployed."

"Jesus," Bree said again, and turned to Tyler. "You didn't know about that?"

"No." The switchblade was still in Tyler's hand, but it was at his side, forgotten. "After I left Vince's place and moved in with Maggie, I never talked to Emma again. Why would I? I had to watch out for myself."

"Yeah," Dave said bitterly, "that's what you do best: look out for yourself. Is that why you came here? To cover your ass and make sure I didn't rat you out to the cops?"

Tyler started to answer, but Bree spoke first. "Why did you run into the house when you saw Tyler?" she asked Dave.

Dave shifted his glower to Bree. "Haven't you been listening? The last time your brother was here he caused a shitstorm. I haven't seen him since then, and he shows up now, out of the blue, this late at night? What was I supposed to think? I wasn't taking any chances on what he might do this time. I didn't know you were also here." Dave raised his eyebrows. "So, why are you here, then? What do you want?"

"Nothing," Tyler said. He closed the switchblade without meeting Bree's eyes. "We should go, Bree. I was wrong."

"Wrong about what?" Dave asked.

Tyler left through the kitchen door without glancing back. Bree's chest loosened as she backed away after him.

"I'm sorry," she said. It was all she could think to say.

"I don't know what Tyler has gotten you into," Dave said, "but he's not a kid anymore, and he's not your responsibility. He's a bad character, and someday he isn't just going to get someone hurt—he's going to get someone killed."

If you only knew, Bree thought miserably.

"Wait," Dave said. "I have to tell you something."

"I have to go—"

"It's about Alissa."

Bree jerked to a stop. "What?"

"I mean, not just about Alissa, but…" He dropped his eyes, realized he was still holding the bat, and set it off to one side. "Other than Tyler, I haven't talked to anyone in your family since that night."

Bree felt the air return to her lungs as her heart rebooted. *That night.* Dave wasn't talking about what was happening now; he was talking about the night at the trailer six months ago. This was the last place she wanted to go right now, but the desperation in his voice was enough to give her pause. Their mother had already told Bree everything, including the detail that Alissa had been born almost nine months after the "affair." The indiscretion between her mother and Dave could barely be called an affair, but rather a one-night stand of confusion, weakness, and alcohol. In the Walker family, almost all problems could be traced back to alcohol.

"I've thought about calling your mother multiple times," Dave said. "I've even picked up the phone, but I can never bring myself to make the call. I want to make things right, but I don't know what to say to her. Everything has been upside down since that night. Did you know that Beth divorced me? I don't expect you to feel sorry for me, but I just wanted to tell you that I've suffered, too. Your mother is as much to blame as I am for cheating. I was trying to do the right thing by coming clean."

Bree's mouth stretched in disgust as she felt a surge of anger, and in that moment, everything from her brother to sister to mother to father was forgotten.

"*That's* what you wanted to tell me?" Bree asked coldly.

"I'm just saying, I'm not the bad guy—"

"My mother didn't leave the trailer that night, but I'm guessing you already know that. She said she wasn't going to be run out of her home, and she would stay and explain things to my father."

Bree felt a wave of nausea as she relived the memory. Bree had begged her mother to call the police, but their mother had refused, saying nothing had happened yet, and maybe nothing would happen. But just to be safe, Bree and Alissa should leave. Bree had taken Alissa to Liz's and drove back to the trailer, but only going as far as the end of the street, where she could wait and watch out of sight. If things did go bad, there was no way Bree was abandoning her mother.

"My father came home to the trailer shortly after that," Bree said tightly. "From where I was parked, I saw him drive his pickup onto the lawn, jump out, and leave the engine running. That's how desperate he was to get inside the trailer to my mother. I ran as fast as I could, and by the time I reached the trailer and went inside, he had already knocked my mother to the floor." Her voice rattled inside her throat. "I grabbed the first thing I saw—the glass coffee pot sitting on the kitchen table—and smashed the side of my father's head with it. It was the only time I've dared fight back against my father, and if he'd been able to get back onto his feet before I got my mother out of there, I think he would have killed me."

Bree saw a wounded flicker in her uncle's eyes, but it brought her no satisfaction.

"So I'm very *sorry* your wife left you, and I'm sorry you feel bad that my mother hasn't reached out to you, but don't try to talk to me about responsibility or character. You had your chance to show your character that night, and that's exactly what you did, because I don't remember you sticking around to take responsibility or to make sure my family stayed safe. I only remember you telling my mother what you had done and then driving off as fast as you could before my father got home."

Bree crossed the kitchen before giving her uncle a chance to respond. As far as she was concerned, there was nothing left to say, and when she glanced back at him, she realized she didn't hate him—not the man who had finally driven their father out of their trailer once and for all—but at the same time, she also couldn't forgive him, because he had torn their family apart. She only felt pity.

For all of them.

CHAPTER THIRTEEN

Tyler was sitting inside the truck with the passenger door open. Liz was standing beside him, trying to talk to him, but Tyler was staring blankly through the windshield, his face pale and gaunt.

"I heard everything from outside the door," Liz said to Bree. "Do you think that girl Emma is okay?"

Tyler's eyes flicked to Bree's. "I think it's time for Liz to go home."

"Go home?" Liz asked. "Why?"

Tyler didn't answer. There was no reason to. They were out of ideas and running out of time. Bree knew this had been a long shot, and now the moment she feared had arrived. They could still go to the police, but if things went bad and the police couldn't find Alissa before midnight, Alissa would be hurt (or worse), but Tyler would stay safe. But if Tyler surrendered himself to the abductor, he would be hurt (or worse), and there was no guarantee they would even release Alissa.

Keep Tyler safe, or risk losing them both. How could anyone in their right mind make that decision?

"Wait a second," Liz said, her eyes growing to the size of saucers as the realization of Tyler's words finally sunk in. "You're trying to get rid of me because you're thinking about giving up to him, aren't you?"

"I caused this," Tyler said, "and I'm the one who has to fix it. All we're doing is wasting time. I've hurt a lot of people in my life, and whatever this is about, I'm sure I deserve it. I don't care anymore. If I can finally do something good, that's what I'm going to do."

"We can still figure this out," Liz sputtered. "I was thinking about this on the way here, and what if it's someone from our school doing this? Brad Whittaker asked Alissa to a movie last month, and she said no. Joslyn Carter thinks that Alissa is after her boyfriend, and Joslyn swore she was going to get Alissa back some way—"

"This isn't some sixteen-year-old doing this, Liz," Bree said. "Someone physically took Alissa against her will, and they're keeping her somewhere. A high-school kid wouldn't have the means to do that."

"You don't know that. Brad's a big guy. I've seen him bench press hundreds of pounds at football practice. We have to keep trying. We can't just let Tyler go off to wherever and let him get hurt. Tell him that, Bree. Tell him!"

Bree grabbed Liz by the arm and dragged her toward the moped. "Come over here—"

"Let go of me!" Liz shouted.

Bree removed her hand, acutely aware of a passing jogger who turned his head at them. Bree raised a hand to the jogger—*everything's okay*—and held a smile until the jogger disappeared from sight.

"Listen to me," Bree said to Liz, checking to make sure Tyler was out of earshot, "I'm not going to let Tyler do anything rash. I promise. We're going to find another way. But I think you're right: it might be someone from Alissa's school."

"You do? But I thought you said—"

"I only said that for Tyler's benefit." She shot a glance over her shoulder at Tyler, who was still inside the truck, waiting for Bree to return. Bree was partially telling the truth: she wasn't about to let Tyler go off and do anything stupid, but she still didn't think it was anyone from Alissa's school. The best way to get rid of Liz was the same way she used to get rid of Alissa as a kid: give her a fake job. Something to do and let them believe they were still helping.

"You have a school yearbook, right?" Bree said "And that has the names and pictures of your classmates?"

"Yes," Liz replied hesitantly.

"Good. Go back to your trailer and get it. I'm going to—"

A door slammed, and Bree snapped her head toward the truck. Tyler had slid into the driver's seat and was leaning out the window, watching them, his face a mask of sorrow. The truck began to move. Tyler was driving away.

"Hey!" Bree shouted.

She broke into a run, going after him, yelling Tyler's name. It was too late. He was already down the street, speeding away in a rush. Bree's heart rose into her throat as she realized she had left her cell phone inside the truck with Tyler.

"He going to call them and go there," Bree said, sprinting back toward Liz. "We have to stop him."

Liz's face went static with shock as she threw one leg over the moped and thumbed the starter. The moped sputtered to life, and by the time Bree reached Liz, the moped was already in motion. Bree hopped on and they sped after Bree's truck.

CHAPTER FOURTEEN

They drove endlessly along back streets, heading in the direction Tyler had taken off in, but there was no sign of Bree's truck. Liz was hunched forward, making arbitrary turns at the end of each street. The night air nipped at Bree's eyes, making them water, and panic welled inside her when the moped began to slow.

"Why are you stopping?" Bree rasped.

"I'm not," Liz said over her shoulder. "It's doing it on its own."

Their speed continued to reduce, until, eventually, the moped sputtered to a stop and died.

"What's wrong?" Bree asked frantically.

"I don't know." Liz tried the starter button. The engine turned over but didn't catch. "I think it overheated."

Bree slid off the moped. "Has this ever happened before?"

It's probably not used to carrying two people." She looked at Bree, horror-stricken. "What are we going to do? We can't let Tyler go there alone. Why did you leave the keys in the truck?"

"I didn't mean to. I never took them out of the ignition when we were watching Dave's house, and when Tyler saw him and ran inside, I followed him without thinking."

"We have to do something," Liz huffed. "I know you don't care what happens to Tyler, but I do."

"Of *course* I care what happens to him. He's my brother—"

"You say that, but if Tyler hadn't gone there on his own, you would have wanted him to go. If it came down to him or Alissa, you'd choose Alissa. Don't say you wouldn't!" Liz's voice broke as it climbed. "I know what you think of Tyler. Alissa tells me. I know you think he's no good, and that he's no better than your father, but you're wrong. He does good things. If I have a problem, he listens to me. And one time he gave me a couple dollars when I really wanted some iced coffee from the store, but I didn't have any money. I've seen sides of him that he hides from other people—sides that he even hides from Alissa. You don't know him like I do!"

Bree was too taken aback to speak. This was the same thing Liz had said about Alissa earlier—*you don't know her like I do*—and while Bree had no doubt Liz knew Alissa better than most people, Tyler was a different story. Tyler wasn't Liz's "friend"—he was her best friend's brother. Most of Alissa's friends had crushed on Tyler at one time or another, and Liz was no exception. But none of Alissa's friends had been around since childhood or were as close to their family as Liz. Only Liz had been there for all the birthday parties, family dinners, Christmas mornings, and sleepovers. Almost every other weekend since kindergarten, where they'd first met, and learned they shared the same middle name, and that pink was their favorite color.

Liz was staring at her feet, refusing to meet Bree's eyes.

"What do you mean by that?" Bree asked with a catch in her throat.

"Nothing."

"Liz—"

"It's nothing," Liz said, her voice barely a whisper. "And it was no one's fault. We never meant it to happen."

"Did Tyler *touch* you?" Bree demanded.

Liz shook her head miserably, not in a way to indicate the answer was no, but rather that Bree wouldn't understand. "It wasn't like that. My dad's new girlfriend had just moved in with us, and my dad was spending all his time with her and ignoring me and acting like he didn't want me around, so I was spending a lot of time at your trailer. Alissa pretended she understood what I was going through, but I don't think she really did. She wasn't close to your father. Not like Tyler was. Tyler understood."

A hard lump formed in Bree's throat.

"I came over to the trailer one night," Liz said, and this time her eyes did find Bree's, but only for a moment. "No one was home, only Tyler. I was upset. I'd been crying most of the day. He was acting funny, and I realized he had been…" Liz stopped herself, but it was too late.

"Drinking," Bree finished for her. Her stomach contracted into a tight, angry ball. "He'd been drinking."

"He wasn't *drunk*," Liz said, as if that somehow made things better. "He was depressed, like me. I… I don't remember why—just that he was. It looked like he had been crying as well."

Bree had only seen Tyler flat out cry once at age sixteen, and that had only been after their father had broken Tyler's arm as punishment for getting into a car accident that had bankrupted the family for months after the fines and damages.

"We started talking. When I started crying again, he…" Liz's head lowered. "He held me. Hugged me. And then… it just sort of… happened. We kissed."

Bree closed her eyes. She could see them in the living room, maybe sitting on the couch, lights dimmed. It wouldn't be that odd for Liz to be there without Alissa. Not really. Liz was always popping over to borrow or return clothes. Snag a soda from the fridge. Hang out and wait for Alissa to get home, passing the time with whoever was there.

"Nothing else happened that night," Liz said, but the defensive note in her voice suggested otherwise.

"*That* night," Bree repeated through numb lips.

She stared stoically at Liz, not waiting for an answer, because there was nothing left to say. Whether it had been only one night or multiple nights, whether it was just kissing or more than that—it changed nothing. Alissa was still gone. Tyler was driving to his fate. And maybe, just maybe, this was the universe's way of balancing itself out. Maybe Tyler did deserve this. Because if it wasn't a sixteen-year-old Liz that Tyler was taking advantage of, it was mother-of-the-year Maggie who dealt drugs, or one of a hundred other girlfriends he had mistreated in some way.

"Call," Liz said, breaking apart Bree's thoughts. "Call and beg them."

At first Bree didn't understand, and before she could ask, Liz took out her own phone and dialed.

"What are you doing?" Bree asked, as if the answer wasn't obvious.

"Calling Alissa's phone."

Bree edged toward Liz, who took a protective step backward, as if Bree might try to rip the phone out of her hands.

"It's ringing," Liz said in a shaky voice. Bree barely heard her over the thudding of her heart. The seconds spun out with no sound. Just as Bree was about to ask if it had gone to voicemail, Liz recoiled, cupped a hand over her mouth, and locked eyes with Bree.

"What?" Bree choked.

"Hello?" Liz said into the phone. "Hello? Can you hear me? If you can, please don't hurt Tyler. Whatever he did, he's sorry, and he didn't mean it, and he'd take it back if he could—"

Bree wrenched the phone from Liz. "This is Bree Walker. I don't know who you are, but Tyler's coming to you, so tell me where I can find Alissa. That was the deal. Tell me."

There was only silence.

"Do we know you?" Bree asked, trying to control the anger and fear in her voice. She needed to know that Alissa was safe; that Tyler hadn't gone off to his unknown fate for no reason.

There were three louds beeps as the call disconnected. As soon as Bree removed the phone from her ear, Liz grabbed it and put it back to hers.

"Hello?" Liz croaked. "Are you still there?"

"They're not," Bree said. There was no time to panic… but if not now, when? Tyler had left them. Whoever had Alissa wasn't going to let her go. Not now. Not ever. Bree understood that now. And it was Bree's fault. All of it. Every wrong choice she had made, every wasted minute… it was all on her.

Liz's phone dinged. Bree shouldered up beside her as Liz raised the phone. The text was from Alissa's number, and on the screen were two words:

Camp Menapace.

CHAPTER FIFTEEN

"And you packed your toothbrush?" Bree asked. "And toothpaste?"

"Yeah," Alissa answered, distracted by their mother, who was running her hand across the wooden totem pole next to the Camp Menapace sign.

"Did you see this?" their mother called out with an enthusiastic grin. "My friends and I always touched this totem for good luck when we got here at the beginning of the week. And did you see the swimming pool? And the archery range?"

This had been going on now for the last five minutes—their mother wandering around the camp, shouting things out, grinning ear to ear as she relived her childhood experiences. Bree was more concerned with Alissa, as this would be her first night away from the house that didn't involve a friend's sleepover or a visit to their grandparents. Alissa was trying to put on a good face, but it was clear she was freaking out on the inside. Bree knew Alissa would enjoy herself once she was settled in (or hoped so, anyway) or it would be a lousy tenth birthday present—not to mention a good chunk of money down the drain.

"And you'll be back to get me Saturday?" Alissa asked. "Before lunchtime?"

Bree winked. "Try and stop me. Mom has to work, so it'll just be me picking you up, but maybe that's for the best."

They both glanced at their mother, who was now parading around the campfire, laughing to herself. It was normally Bree's job to drive Alissa around on the weekends—leaving their mother free to clean, run errands, and do other odds and ends she couldn't normally do during the week—but their mother had insisted on coming, and now Bree understood why. It had been a while since Bree had seen their mother so joyful, and it made her heart swell. Their mother needed some joy in her life. So did Bree, for that matter. Hopefully her turn was coming.

"I hope you don't have to pee," Liz said, nudging up beside Alissa and waving a hand toward the bathrooms in the distance. "The bathroom smells like sh—" She caught herself and smiled at Bree. "Like stinky poop."

"Uh-huh," Bree said, raising an eyebrow. She had hoped Alissa would embark on this adventure without Liz, but the two were inseparable, and Alissa would only go if Liz came along. It wasn't that Bree didn't like Liz; it was that Liz was adventurous and quick to get into trouble by not thinking things through. There was still dried blood on Alissa's carpet from the time Liz had generously offered to pierce Alissa's ears using a needle and an ice cube. Not to mention the burn marks on the kitchen floor from the time the two of them lit sparklers inside the trailer. Fortunately, the two hadn't gotten into any sort of serious trouble, but Alissa (by nature) was a follower, and that worried Bree to no end.

"I see you and Lizzy found each other," their mother said, finally finished with her self-guided tour. "Are you girls just so excited? Lizzy, did you know I used to come here as a little girl? Those were four of the best summers of my life. Bree always wanted to come, but it never worked out."

That was putting it mildly. Bree had begged and pleaded for three summers in a row, but money had been tight back then (even more so than now), and their father had been dead set against the idea. Waste of a week and money, he had said. If Bree wants to go that bad, she can work there for the summer. Their father also hadn't been keen on Alissa going, but their mother had eventually worn him down. Bree suspected it had something to do with all the overtime their mother had worked in the months leading up to it.

"We should go," Liz said, pulling on the crook of Alissa's arm. "They're getting ready to let people into the cabins and we want to get in line so we can choose our bunks."

Alissa resisted Liz's attempt to be dislodged, clearly not ready to go. "Can Tyler also come when you pick me up? I wish he had been home so I could have said goodbye. Can you ask him if he'll come?"

"I can and will," Bree promised, knowing the chances of Tyler wanting to come (or even being around to ask) were slim to none. At the beginning of the summer, Tyler had developed a habit of coming and going as he pleased, rarely asking permission, and often staying overnight at "friends'" houses. Their mother had come down fairly hard on him at first, but after the fifth, sixth, and seven occurrences, it became clear Tyler had no intention of changing his ways, and their mother had given up. There were more important things to worry about than what her fifteen-year-old son was doing those nights, because surely it was nothing more than playing video games or watching movies.

"Ready?" Liz asked, continuing to tug at Alissa, whose eyes stayed locked on Bree's.

"Hey, Mom," Bree said, "why don't you walk Liz to the cabin and Alissa and I will be along in a minute. I'd like to talk to Alissa alone… if that's okay with you, Alissa."

Alissa was nodding before Bree finished. "Yeah. I mean, I guess so. If you have to."

"Have you seen the dining hall?" their mother asked Liz, leading her away. "They have a moose head on the wall that the head counselor kisses at the end of the week. It's hysterical."

Bree waited until their mother and Liz were out of earshot before squatting before Alissa. "Talk to me."

"I want to be here," Alissa said, the words pouring from her mouth in a hushed voice, "and I know you and Mom paid a lot for this, and I'll have a lot of fun… but…"

Bree waited as Alissa looked over her shoulder. Not toward Liz and their mother, but rather a sweeping gesture of the entire camp.

"What if I have to go to the bathroom in the middle of the night, or what if the other kids don't like me, or what if they laugh at me because I can't swim, or—"

"Hey," Bree said, poking Alissa's stomach, "none of that is going to happen. I mean, waking up in the middle of the night to pee probably will, because we both know you have the bladder the size of a pumpkin seed."

Bree had hoped for a smile, but Alissa only stared, waiting for something more. Now wasn't the time for jokes. Bree had never been an anxious child, had never overthought things or worried the way Alissa did, and Bree often had to remind herself that not everyone thought, felt, and reacted in the same way.

"Listen to me," Bree said, as she had said a hundred times before, "you're a Walker, just like me, and because of that—as you know—we each have our own awesome superpower. What's my superpower?"

"Watching out for me," Alissa said.

"And Tyler's?"

A small grin. "Being purposefully difficult."

"Darn tooting. And yours?"

"Being brave," Alissa said with a resigned sigh, "but you're the only one who says that, and it's not true."

"Are you kidding me? You're the bravest kid I know. I say that to everyone I meet."

Alissa eyed her suspiciously. "No you don't."

"I absolutely do. Remember last month when you didn't want to go to the dentist, but you did anyway?"

"Yeah…"

"That's being brave." Bree lowered her voice. "When I was your age, I used to hide when it was time to go to the dentist. I was terrified. Mom always had to drag me there, kicking and screaming, and even then, I refused to open my mouth until they made me."

"That's not true," Alissa said doubtfully. "Is it?"

"Swear. And what about that time at the park when that boy took that little girl's toy away from her and she started to cry? You

marched up to that bully, took it out of his hands, and gave it back to the girl."

A frown creased Alissa's forehead. "But he wasn't a bully; he was her brother."

"But you didn't know that. And sure... that kid's mother chewed me out for what you did, but you know what? I didn't care. You saw someone in trouble, and you were brave and did the right thing. That's huge. I was so proud of you." Bree tucked a loose strand of Alissa's hair behind her ear. "You are brave, Alissa, and I know this is new and scary, but once Mom and I are outta here, I have no doubt your superpowers will leap into action."

Alissa didn't look entirely convinced, but her brow had smoothed and her shoulders had relaxed. Alissa looked across the camp at their mother, who was chattering away at Liz as they waited in line with other campers and parents.

"You should probably use those powers to save Liz from Mom," Bree said.

Alissa gave Bree a quick hug, then checked to make sure no one had seen. "See you Saturday."

"Wouldn't miss it for the world."

Alissa trudged off toward Liz and their mother, her tiny frame swaying side to side from the weight of her bag. Liz looked beyond relieved to have Alissa back, and Bree started toward their car to wait for their mother, dragging a hand across the totem pole as she passed, knowing everything was going to be okay—

"There!" Liz exclaimed, her voice just above the scream of the moped's muffler. "I see it!"

Bree blinked back tears from the cool night air as she looked ahead over Liz's shoulder and saw the CAMP MENAPACE sign. It had taken ten minutes before the moped had finally started, and at least another thirty minutes to get here. Without her phone, she didn't know the exact time but guessed it to be almost eleven o'clock. Bree had no idea if midnight still had significance, but until Alissa was safely back in her arms, she wasn't going to assume anything.

There was a metal gate across the road into the camp with an affixed sign: NO TRESPASSING. The owners had filed for bankruptcy almost four years ago, and the ground had stood empty since. Bree remembered hearing about a few acts of vandalism on the news, which was no surprise since the gate was nothing more than two slender, metal arms that met in the middle with a padlock—just enough to stop a vehicle, but not much else. Liz killed the motor but left the headlight on. The totem pole at the edge of the parking lot was just visible, and the cabins were dark shapes in the distance, lit only by the bright moon of the cloudless night sky. The only sounds were the chirp of crickets and the rustling of trees in the wind.

"Now what?" Liz asked as they both dismounted.

That was the million-dollar question. "You stayed at this camp for a week. If Alissa is here, she has to be locked away in a building or in a basement or something. Are there any basements here? Any cellars? Something with a concrete floor and walls?"

Liz gave a tentative shrug. "I don't think so, but it was six years ago, and I only came that one summer with Alissa—"

"Think. Other than the cabins, what other buildings are here?"

"Uh… bathrooms, the dining hall… There was a camp store where we would buy things like candy…" Liz trailed off with another shrug. "That's most of what I remember."

Bree rattled the gate's arms. The padlock jiggled but held firm.

"Do we walk?" Liz asked.

Bree looked down the road and then back at the moped. She went to it, gripped it by the handlebars, and lowered it onto its side.

"We'll need more than just the light from your phone to see," she told Liz. "Help me pull it."

It took a moment for Liz to understand, but as soon as Bree ducked down and started dragging the moped underneath the waist-high arms of the gate, Liz grabbed the other handlebar and pulled with her. When the moped was on the other side and clear of the arms, Bree righted it with a grunt.

"Here," Bree said, leaning the moped toward Liz, who took it by the handlebars. "You push, and I'll walk beside you. It's your job to point the headlight where I tell you. Okay?"

Liz turned on the headlight. "Okay."

They started down the road toward the camp, Liz walking the moped as Bree padded silently beside her, trying to look everywhere at once. A branch snapped in the distance, and Bree told herself it was a roaming deer, nothing more. She had never been afraid of the dark, not even as a child, but being out here—and under these circumstances—had put even the hairs on the back of her neck on edge. She couldn't imagine being here alone without Liz. Luckily for Bree, Liz was a tenacious little shit who hadn't listened to Bree's continuous demands to stop following and go home.

"That's the office," Liz said as they neared the parking lot. Bree remembered that much about the camp layout: the office was set off to the right, just past the totem pole, where they had checked Alissa in upon arrival. The building itself was still in good shape, but all the windows had been broken, and ugly weeds smothered the brick path that led to the front door.

"Alissa!" Liz shouted, eliciting a startled cry from Bree.

"Hey," Bree said. "I don't know if that's a good idea—"

"How else are we going to find her? If Alissa's here, she'll hear us, won't she? She'll hear us and call out, and then we can find her."

Liz had a point. Again. The camp was spread out over a large area, and even if it was daytime (and their visibility was better), it would still be difficult to search everything—especially since they didn't know what they were looking for.

"Unless she can't answer," Liz added in a thin voice.

Bree didn't want to let her mind go there. The abductor had sent them to a campsite that was abandoned and secluded, with acres upon acres of ground for burying things. Anything could happen out here. Anything could have already happened out here.

"We can't think like that," Bree said. "Whoever has Alissa said she wouldn't be hurt if Tyler went to them. And he did. They told us to come here for a reason, and that reason is to find Alissa. Do you understand me? Alissa is here, waiting for us—counting on us. She has to be here, because this is the only place we *know* to be."

Bree's voice cracked at the end, and she turned away from Liz with a sharp breath. Now wasn't the time to unravel. She had held it together this long, and she could hold it together a while longer. They were so close. Bree could feel it.

"There's a map," Liz said, jerking the moped to a stop. "That wasn't there when we came here."

Liz turned the handlebars and lit the map with her headlight. It was the size of a movie poster, encapsulated within a wooden box and protected behind glass. The buildings were cartoon drawings with red lettering stating what each structure was, and Bree wiped dust and grime from the glass for a better look. A large, red X marked the main office, and beyond that were paths that led to the surrounding buildings. There were maybe fifteen or twenty. Not impossible, but in the darkness it would take a bit of time.

"Bathhouse," Bree read under her breath. "Stables. Ropes course. Health center. Pool." She glanced at Liz. "What's this building marked pavilion? Do you remember?"

Liz only shook her head.

Bree stepped back and surveyed the camp spread out ahead of them.

"What do we do?" Liz asked.

"The only thing we can do," Bree answered. "We search until we find her."

"And if we don't find her?"

Bree had no answer for that.

CHAPTER SIXTEEN

Splitting up would have allowed them to cover twice as much ground, but since the moped headlight was their main source of light, they had to work together: Liz walked the moped to light the path, and when they came to a building, Bree would go inside and use the flashlight on Liz's cell phone for a better look. They had managed to cover the entire camp this way, but aside from soiled mattresses, broken glass, and lots and lots of animal droppings, there was no sign that anyone had been inside these buildings for years. And nothing they had seen suggested the possibility of a basement or underground structure with concrete floors and walls.

"Alissa's not here," Liz said as Bree emerged after checking the last cabin. "There's no reason for us not to call the police now. You said you didn't want to earlier because you were worried that whoever took Alissa would hurt her, but you also said you believed they wouldn't hurt her if they got Tyler, and now they have Tyler, but we don't have Alissa."

"We can't," Bree said. "Not until we have Alissa. Not until we know for sure she's free and safe of whoever has her."

"So we just trust whatever this person says? You brought us here because they sent a text with the name of this camp. It didn't even say to come here. We don't even know if that picture was taken here. It could have been taken anywhere."

Bree took the photograph from her pocket and held it in front of Liz's face.

"If you tell anyone, she dies," Bree said hoarsely. "Do you see those words? Because I do. And I believe them."

"I do, too, but you can't keep pretending that Tyler is going to be okay, because he's not. They want him for a reason—"

"Because of something Tyler did!" Bree spat. Her voice echoed through the trees and spiraled into the distance. "They want Tyler because of something *he* did, and we can guess what might happen to him, but we *know* what will happen to Alissa if we don't do what they say." The photograph trembled in Bree's hand. "We know, because it says so right here, and I'm not taking any chances. Not one. I don't want anything to happen to either of them, but if it comes down to Tyler or Alissa…"

Bree was too horrified at the thought to finish.

"Tyler caused this," Bree said again with a catch in her throat, "and Tyler can take care of himself more than Alissa, who is sixteen and has been missing for two days. I didn't ask you to come with me. I told you to stay home, and you didn't listen, and now we're here, and I'm doing the best I can. And if they say Alissa is here, she is. And we will find her, and when we do that, *then* we can worry about Tyler."

Bree turned away from Liz, blinking back tears and refusing to cry. Alissa was here because she *had* to be here. There was nowhere else.

She caught sight of another map and went to it, holding her light to the glass. This red X showed they were near the middle of the camp, and she scanned the surrounding buildings for anything they might have missed, any structures or areas off the beaten path.

"We didn't check the swimming pool," Bree said over her shoulder as she fingered the glass. "Or the stables."

Liz rolled up behind her, lighting the map with the moped headlight. "The swimming pool is on the other side, past the campfire, but it's just a pool. There's nothing else. And the stables are just a few barns—"

"What's 'riflery'?" Bree asked, pointing to it on the map. "A shooting range?"

"I guess. Alissa and I never did that. I don't even know if that was here when we were."

The map showed the path to riflery past the dining hall, and Bree started briskly in that direction, holding the light steady as Liz followed on the moped. The path began to spiral downward away from the main camp, and within seconds, they were surrounded by thick bush on both sides. Up ahead was a wooden sign—RIFLERY—sitting at the edge of a large, open field. When Liz pulled up behind Bree, the field lit up, and Bree's skin prickled.

An SUV was parked in the grass on the other side, facing away from them. All the windows were rolled up. It didn't look like anyone was inside, but it was impossible to tell from this distance.

"Why is that here?" Liz whispered.

Bree moved slowly toward the SUV, looking in all directions and listening for sounds, and stopped just shy of the driver-side door. Liz was saying Bree's name, telling her to be careful. Bree wet her lips as she lifted the lit phone to the window. The driver and passenger seat were empty. In the console between them was an unopened bottle of water.

"I don't like this," Liz said.

Bree did a quick check of the back seats—also empty—before opening the driver-side door. Light flooded out from inside, and the SUV began to ding. The keys were hanging from the ignition. Bree reached in with a quick burst, yanked them out to end the noise, and quickly backed away. She glanced around to see if the noise had summoned anyone, or anything, before looking at the key ring in her hand. There were two other keys next to the ignition key: what looked to be a house key, and a small, silver key. The only other thing attached was a tiny, blue teddy bear made of plastic.

Liz kick-standed the moped but kept a fixed distanced. "Why did they leave the keys?"

"I don't know," Bree said absently, checking the surroundings again, trying to make sense of it. She didn't know much about vehicles, but this SUV looked fairly new—maybe even last year's model. It didn't have license plates, only a "registration applied for" notice in the back window. This wasn't a relic that had been abandoned or left here by the previous camp owners. Then again, maybe that's all it was—the previous or current owners storing their vehicle. Or maybe someone else had been here just for fun and the SUV wouldn't start or it had run out of gas. But that didn't explain the keys. No, keys dangling from an ignition meant either something had gone wrong for someone, or someone was momentarily doing something... and would return.

"This has to be connected to Alissa," Bree said. "It's the only thing out here besides us that doesn't belong. But why is it here? And who drove it out here?"

"What if that someone's out here right now?" Liz asked in a hushed voice. "What if they're off doing something—something they don't want us to know about—and when they come back and find us..."

Bree absently pushed the keys into her pocket as she circled to the front of the SUV and placed a hand on the hood. It was cool to the touch, which meant it hadn't been running recently. The path continued in front of the SUV, winding and widening, as if there was another road that led out of the camp.

"We have to *go*," Liz moaned. "Bree, this is freaking me out—"

"Be quiet."

"What are you doing?" Liz rasped as Bree leaned into the driver's side. Bree turned on the headlights, lighting up the area ahead of them, and there, just a short distance away and buried halfway inside a sloping hill, was a concrete wall with a thick, metal door.

"Oh, shit," Bree said.

"What?"

Bree bolted toward the door on wobbly legs.

Liz caught Bree by the arm, momentarily stopping her. "We don't know what's in there," Liz said.

"Alissa's in there. Don't you get it? This is the place. It's some sort of bomb shelter from years and years ago, which means the floors and walls are made of concrete. This is where he's keeping Alissa—"

"But what if that's his SUV and he's also in there?" Liz asked. "We don't have anything to protect ourselves with!"

Bree wavered, but only for a moment. "If he's in there, I'll claw his eyes out to get to Alissa."

Bree shook her arm free and went to the door. The blue paint had dulled and flaked over the years, and the hinges were blistered with rust. Dangling from the U-shaped handle was a large, shiny, unlocked padlock. She gripped the handle with both hands and leaned back. For a horrible moment she thought it wasn't going to budge, and then, very slowly on groaning hinges, the door began to open. The door was easily three inches thick and weighed hundreds of pounds, and as much as she wanted to slip inside when it was halfway open, she realized she needed as much light from the SUV's headlights as she could get. There wasn't a room directly inside but six concrete steps, leading down. At the bottom was a short, concrete hallway, leading farther into the ground.

There was an intense blast of light as Liz drove the moped to a stop behind Bree, flooding the inside of the shelter with additional light.

"Alissa!" Bree called out.

The word vibrated against the walls before spiraling away into nothingness. There was no response, not at first, and then a muffled: "Here!"

Bree's remaining bit of sanity broke. She lunged down the steps, the phone's flashlight splashing light left and right against the walls, and paused when she saw another closed metal door at the end of the short hallway.

"I'm coming!" Bree hollered, her heart rate increasing with every step. "Alissa!"

Bree reached the door. It had no lock, only a handle that twisted. Bree turned it and yanked open the door.

And there, on the floor in the corner, sitting next to a large camping lamp that filled the room with light, was a girl Bree had never seen before in her life.

CHAPTER SEVENTEEN

"What?" Liz gasped. She was in the hallway behind Bree, clutching onto the back of Bree's shirt. "Who's that?"

Bree had no answer. Shock had stolen her voice. The girl remained on the floor, head raised, her long, unruly blonde hair tucked behind her ears. Her eyes were red and swollen and her face was heavy with fatigue. She couldn't be more than eighteen or nineteen.

"Help her," Liz said frantically.

The girl shrank at Liz's words, but they awakened Bree, who had been stunned into submission. Bree edged toward the girl with one hand in the air. "We're not going to hurt you."

"I need my phone," the girl said. Her voice was high, almost reedy. "It's in my car."

"*Your* car?" Bree repeated. "That's your SUV out there?"

"Yes."

"How did you get here? Who did this to you? Who are you?"

The girl only lowered her head. "I need my phone."

"We have a phone," Liz said, taking it from Bree's hand. "We can call—"

"No! I have to call him from my phone!"

"Call who?" Bree asked.

"Bree," Liz said. "Look."

Bree dragged her eyes away from the girl to where Liz was pointing. In the opposite corner were canned foods, cereal, and bottles of water. Above that, two cots were affixed to the wall. Both cots had blankets… and both sets were a crumpled mess.

"Alissa was here," Bree said.

The girl nodded. "Yes."

"Is she hurt?" Bree asked, her feet nudging her forward. "Where is she? Alissa's my sister."

"She's not hurt, but he took her. He came and took her from here, maybe an hour ago."

"Where? Where did he take her?"

When the girl didn't answer, all the blood rushed to Bree's head. "We don't have time for this. I know you're scared, but you need to tell us what you know. My sister is out there with a maniac—"

"He's not a maniac," the girl said, her voice all at once teetering on the edge of anger, "he's just hurt and angry, and you would be too if someone hurt your family."

All the air left Bree's lungs. "*Who's* angry and hurt?"

The girl's eyes were wet with tears, but her mouth was an angry slit, and her upper lip trembled. If looks could kill, Bree would have been dead where she stood.

"You're with him," Bree said tonelessly. "You're helping the person… the *man* who took Alissa. You're a part of this."

The girl's brow softened. "I'm not helping him."

"I don't understand," Liz said, cutting her eyes from the girl to Bree. "If she's with him, why is she in here? Why didn't she just leave? Both of the doors into this place were unlocked."

There was another flash of emotion on the girl's face—anger, remorse, maybe both—as she leaned forward and worked herself to her feet using her hands. Bree heard it before she saw it—the rattle of a small chain, one end affixed to the leg of the lower cot and the other end shackled to the girl's ankle by a small padlock.

"I'm not helping him," the girl said again, "but I can help you. Do you want me to beg? Then I'm begging you. Please… *please*… get me my phone. It's in the glovebox."

There was no way to know if the girl was telling the truth, but there was only one way to find out.

"Get the phone," Bree said to Liz.

"Is Tyler going to die?' Liz said to the girl.

The girl's face softened. "I don't know."

That was enough to get Liz moving. She hurried out the door and up the concrete steps into the night.

"Was Tyler here?" Bree asked, her voice pained. "Who's doing this and why? Why do you have to call him? Why did he chain and leave you here?"

"I can't."

Bree's skin tightened. "What do you mean you can't?"

"He gave me instructions. He told me I can't answer any questions. He said if I... if *we* followed his instructions exactly, no one would be hurt."

"And you believe that?"

The girl's lips pursed. "We have no choice."

"I got it," Liz said, slightly out of breath, holding out the phone. Bree grabbed it out of Liz's hand as the girl reached for it.

"What are you doing?" Liz balked.

Bree tapped the screen. "What's the passcode?"

Liz's head went back and forth between Bree and the girl. "She isn't the bad guy, Bree. She's chained up—"

"And until she tells me the code, she's going to stay chained up." Heat flooded Bree's face as she turned on Liz. "Don't you get it? This isn't some girl who was also abducted and left here—she's a part of this. She knows who took Alissa and where Tyler is, and she's going to tell us. Or else."

"Or else *what*?" Liz asked warily.

"I tried to stop him," the girl said, her voice filling the room, "and because of that, he did this to me."

"Who did?" Bree demanded. "*Who* did this to you?"

"I already told you," the girl said, "I can't—"

"I don't believe you. You say you want to help, but you refuse to tell me. Why should we believe anything you say? Why should we believe Alissa was even here?"

"Right there," the girl said, jabbing a shaky finger at the far corner. "Alissa was there, rocking and shivering and sobbing uncontrollably. She wasn't hurt, but she had peed through her jeans and hadn't eaten for twenty-four hours. She was terrified, and the only person she had was me. *Me.* I was the one who was here to comfort her and tell her everything was going to be okay. She kept asking me who I was and why I was here, but I couldn't tell her the truth." The girl's eyes began to shine. "So I lied to her. I lied and told her that I had also been abducted, because it was the only way I could help, and I *wanted* to help, because I don't want Alissa hurt, and I don't want Tyler hurt. I know you have no reason to trust me, but I'm all you have, so you can either give me my phone or we can sit here and do this. If I say anything more and he finds out, he *will* hurt them. We have to do what he says."

The girl's voice had gone hoarse and her chin was trembling. A thousand more questions jumbled Bree's tongue, each more troubling than the last.

"What do we do, Bree?" Liz asked.

Bree held out the phone. "Make the call."

CHAPTER EIGHTEEN

It only took a moment to figure out something wasn't right. The girl had dialed the phone, put it to her ear, pulled it away, frowned, and dialed again.

"What's wrong?" Liz asked.

"Nothing," the girl said. She tapped at the screen again and put the phone to her ear. Bree inched closer, just barely able to hear the ringing, which was then followed by a generic voicemail.

Dread filled Bree's gut. "Why isn't he answering? What does that mean?"

"I don't know. He told me to call him on his phone when you got here, and after that, he would tell us what to do next. I don't know why he isn't answering… but I can find him."

"What do you mean, you can *find* him?"

"I can figure out where he took Alissa. I know I can." The girl looked at her ankle. "We need the key to the padlock."

"Where is it?" Bree asked.

"I don't know. He was supposed to tell me when I called." Her gaze shifted to Liz. "Did you see a key inside my SUV when you got my phone? Maybe on the seat or on the floor?"

"No," Liz said, "but Bree found the car keys."

They both looked at Bree. Bree fished the ring from her pocket and held up the small key.

"That key wasn't on there when I drove here," the girl said.

"Of course it wasn't," Bree said. "I'm sure *he* put it on there after he locked you in, right? Because that makes about as much sense as everything else you're telling us."

"What are you saying?" Liz asked.

"I'm saying this is a waste of our time," Bree said to Liz. "This girl's told us next to nothing except she's supposed to make a phone call when we got here. She's just a pawn in this like we are, and we have no reason to trust her or believe anything she says. Come on, Liz."

Bree started for the door.

"You're leaving me?" the girl choked.

"Bree," Liz said, "we can't just go—"

"We don't need her," Bree said over her shoulder. "We have her phone. Whoever took Alissa will eventually call, and when they do, we'll figure out how to trace the number. We have this girl's car keys, so we can even take her SUV. If she won't give us any answers, then she can stay in here and starve for all I care. For all we know, she's the one who took Alissa. Let's go, Liz."

The girl's remaining composure broke. "I'm not doing this; it's my stepfather, Shane! He took Alissa, and if you don't let me out here, he's going to hurt Tyler!"

And just like that, there it was.

Stepfather.

"Why?" Bree asked, her voice a shard of glass. "What does he want with Tyler?"

The girl was crying, hands to her face. Bree advanced on the girl, who immediately cowered back in fear, tripped over her feet, and tumbled backward onto the cot.

"Don't hurt her," Liz stammered.

"I'm not," Bree said without turning as she bent down, held the girl's ankle steady in one hand, and tried to slide the key into the padlock. "I was bluffing about leaving you. Hold still."

The girl calmed, just barely, but stopped moving long enough for Bree to unlock it. As soon as the chain fell to the floor, the girl jerked her legs into her chest and hugged them.

"I know you're scared," Bree said, "but if you really want to help Tyler and Alissa, you need to pull yourself together and tell me everything. Do you understand?"

The girl made a whimpering sound. Her head stayed buried in her knees, muffling her hiccuping sobs, and when Liz crept forward, Bree waved her back.

"You said you can figure out where he is," Bree said, lowering her voice in the hopes the girl would quiet to hear Bree's words. "What did you mean by that?"

The girl's eyes, awash with tears, poked out above her knees. "He…" She sniffed. "My stepfather owns a few businesses and properties. He bought this camp when it closed a few years ago but hasn't decided what to do with it yet. He also recently bought an old brewery that's sitting vacant in the middle of nowhere. He wants to open a restaurant there."

Bree didn't need to hear anymore. "You think that's where he took Alissa, and where he told Tyler to go?"

"It has to be. I don't know where it is, but I think I could figure it out if I get on his computer at the house."

"The house?" Liz asked.

The girl dropped her eyes. "Yes. We… I live there. With him."

"You live with him," Bree said, feeling a crawl of disgust. "And your mother? Is she a part of this, too?"

"My mother died last year."

"What are we waiting for?" Liz asked. "Let's go there."

The girl remained where she was. Liz and Bree exchanged a glance.

"You said you want to help," Bree said in a growing fever of impatience, "so this is how you do it. We go there and you tell me everything. It's the only way to help Alissa and Tyler."

"And my stepfather? You'll help him, too?"

Bree blinked, not understanding at first. "What?"

"I know you have no reason to believe me, but my stepfather isn't a maniac. He's isn't. There's so much more you don't understand that I can't explain, but I know I can talk some sense into him before anyone gets hurt. There's no reason for him to go to jail."

"My brother's and sister's lives are in danger," Bree said, "and you're worried about your stepfather going to jail? How do you think this is going to end? We're all going to walk away and pretend none of this happened?"

Bree stopped herself as the girl's face began to twitch and pull. It was insanity for this girl to think her stepfather could get away with what he had done without any repercussions, but if she really was the only link to finding Alissa, Bree would tell her whatever she wanted to hear.

"Okay," Bree said. "We do it your way. I promise to do what I can to also help your stepfather... if my family hasn't been hurt."

A look of uncertainty passed over the girl's face. "You mean that? You're not just saying that?"

"I mean it."

Liz took a step back as the girl slid off the cot, tucked her bangs behind her eyes, and stared at her feet. No one spoke or moved, and finally—mostly because Bree had no idea what was supposed to happen next—Bree held out the SUV keys. The girl took them with a tentative nod and started for the exit.

"What's your name?" Liz asked.

The girl stopped, turned, and took a papery breath.

She said, "I'm Emma."

CHAPTER NINETEEN

Bree sat as stiff as a board in the passenger seat of the SUV, Liz in the back seat, and Emma at the wheel. *Emma*. The girl Tyler had been dating before Maggie, who had followed Tyler and made the scene at Dave's house.

"Shane's phone is still going to voicemail," Emma said, returning the phone to the console. "I don't know why—"

"It wasn't Tyler's fault," Bree said abruptly. "I know he hurt you and you were upset and crashed your car, but if that's the reason your stepfather is doing this to my family, that's beyond insane."

Bree waited for Emma to speak, or turn, or breathe, or do or say anything, but Emma only stared straight ahead with both hands gripping the wheel.

"I'm sorry for what my brother did," Bree said, "and Tyler's sorry for what he did. If he could take it back, he would."

"I know, but what's done is done. I should have never gotten involved with Tyler, but I was lonely, and I knew he wasn't looking for anything serious, and we were only together a few weeks…" Emma sniffled. "I still thought we had something special. He made me feel special. But maybe that's what he does to all the girls. Makes them feel special."

Liz made a sound, and Bree glanced over her shoulder into the back seat. Liz was burning holes into the back of Emma's seat, arms crossed, a sneer on her lips. As if the situation wasn't already delicate enough, this was all Bree needed: a jealous sixteen-year-old to throw into the mix.

Bree waited for more, but Emma only stared out the windshield. The houses were growing sparser now, lots of fields and open space, and up ahead was what appeared to be their destination. The house was a large three-story, and like the SUV, very new. The driveway alone was easily twice the length of Bree's trailer, and a shiny new boat sat off to the side, alongside an ATV. A dog was running up to greet them, barking and bucking. Bree leaned back in her seat as the SUV came to a stop and the dog jumped onto the passenger window. It was panting heavily but clearly excited, not angry.

"That's Christina," Emma said, killing the engine. "She's named after my mother. I got her last year. She's friendly. She won't hurt you."

Emma climbed out, and Bree waited for the dog to circle to the driver's side before warily opening her door. There were no other vehicles in the driveway and no other houses in sight. The night air was crisp with a low breeze.

"I don't like this," Liz said petulantly, dropping her voice to a confidential whisper. "And I don't trust this girl. Not at all."

Emma was unlocking the front door to the house as Christina sat on her haunches, watching and panting. Bree straightened as Emma motioned in their direction—*come on*.

"I don't trust her either," Bree said, "but we don't have any other choice. We also don't both have to do this."

"What do you mean?"

"I want you to stay here, outside. Or better yet, lock yourself inside the SUV. You have your phone. You're our lifeline to the outside world."

"But—"

"If someone drives up, call the police. If you hear screaming from inside the house, call the police. If someone runs outside from the house carrying a chainsaw—"

"I get it," Liz said, "I should call the police. But shouldn't we call the police now? We know who has Alissa, and we know where they live. The police can take it from here."

Bree took Liz by the shoulders. "Listen to me carefully. Nothing has changed. You said so yourself: we can't trust her. We don't know if anything she's telling us is the truth, and even if she is, we still don't know where her stepfather is, or where he has Alissa and Tyler. Our only chance is to see this through and hope and pray Emma is telling the truth and wants to help." Bree wet her lips. "You have to promise me you won't call the police. Not yet. We don't call until there's no other choice. Do you hear me?"

"Yes," Liz said with a wince. "You're pinching my arm."

Bree released her grip and looked over her shoulder toward the house. Emma and the dog had disappeared inside.

"Everything is going to be okay," Bree said. "I know it is. And before we know it, Alissa and Tyler are going to be back in our reach. Okay?"

Liz gave a fervent nod. "Okay."

Bree lingered a moment longer to gather her fortitude, then started toward the house. Whatever happened next was out of Bree's hands… and that was the most terrifying thought of all.

CHAPTER TWENTY

The front door opened into a large foyer with high ceilings, bare walls, and marbled flooring. The interior was cold and impersonal but hardly the habitat of a deranged lunatic. An old grandfather clock stood guard by the staircase, and a wilted plant sat in the far corner like a sulking toddler who had been sent to time-out.

This is where he lives.

The thought looped endlessly inside Bree's head. This was where he lived. Where he ate. Slept. For all Bree knew, he could be here now, maybe just around the corner, waiting to leap out…

She shuddered at the thought, but there was no turning back now.

The dog was lying by an open doorway to the left, head rested between its paws, watching Bree without interest. Bree could hear Emma inside the room, shuffling through papers and talking under her breath. From where Bree was standing, she could see a wall of wooden bookshelves in the background, filled with books of all shapes, sizes, and colors. It was a study.

The dog lifted its eyes as Bree moved past. Emma was poised over a laptop behind a small desk. The bookshelves Bree had spied from the entrance ran the length of the wall and were tall enough to necessitate a wooden ladder on wheels that sat at the end. A cold finger traced Bree's spine as she caught sight of a gold-framed picture on the middle shelf, tilted sideways, of a man and woman. The woman had to be Emma's mother (same stringy blonde hair, sharp jawline, and high forehead), which meant the man had to be Emma's stepfather. He was nothing like Bree expected: average-looking, probably in his forties, with thick, wavy hair and a dark beard. Someone you might pass on the street without a second thought. But wasn't that the way it always was? Weren't most murderers and kidnapers kind and quiet and unassuming in the daily lives?

"I never knew my real father," Emma said. "He left my mother shortly after I was born. They weren't married or anything; it was just some guy she was dating at the time." Emma's voice dropped. "I don't think my mother really wanted me either. She was barely around when I was growing up, always leaving me with babysitters, always going out on dates. We always had food and a place to live, but only because my mother always had someone taking care of us. I know my mother always wanted to be married, but she was always looking for a rich guy. I know that sounds terrible, but it's the truth. When I was fourteen, she met Shane and they got married. Last year, my mother got pregnant with what would have been my half-brother, and she died giving birth to him."

There was a noise from the entrance, and Bree turned, expecting to see Shane in the doorway. But it was only the dog, padding into the room, its nails clicking the hardwood floor as it went to Emma.

"Shane wasn't the same after that," Emma said. She was still typing, but her fingers had slowed, and her face seemed to sag. "All he wanted was a child of his own. He grew up in foster homes and never knew his parents, and until he met my mother, he never had any family." Her eyes slid briefly to Bree's before going back to the screen. "I know you don't care about these things, but I'm just trying to help you see that he's not a maniac, as you called him."

Emma clicked the mouse twice, leaned back, and turned the laptop toward Bree.

Bree inched forward until she could see the screen. It was an e-mail between Shane and someone named Paul Varengo. The subject line was Uhlman Industries. Bree quickly scanned the message. Something about a building, newly acquired by Emma's father, and there was an issue with something called revenue stamps when they tried to file some paperwork.

"This is the place you were talking about earlier," Bree said. "You think this is where he's keeping Alissa? You think this is where Tyler went?"

"Yes. The problem is that I don't know where it's at. I'm not even sure if it's in this town. I tried to search online to find the address, but I don't know what the brewery was called, so there's nothing to go on—just this e-mail and what I heard Shane say about it. I tried doing a search on Uhlman Industries, but that just took me to a corporate webpage." Emma picked up her phone and dialed. "There's something else I can try."

"Who are you calling?" Bree asked.

"Paul Varengo. He's Shane's business partner." She started to say more but then tilted the phone closer to her mouth. "Paul, this is Emma Lockhart. I need you to call me back. It's an emergency. Thank you."

"Does he know about this?" Bree asked in disgust as Emma ended the call. "About what your stepfather has done?"

"No. And Paul will call me back soon. He always answers his phone, and when he doesn't, it never takes long to return the call. He might be in a late-night meeting, or on another call or something. We just have to wait."

A few second passed in silence. Emma closed the laptop. Her hands stayed on top as she stared into the picture of her mother and stepfather.

"My mother married Shane four years ago, and he loved her with all his heart... but he didn't love me. He was never mean or cruel, just indifferent. He played the part of the stepfather, but there was no love there. I think even my mother knew it, but it wasn't like she was going to leave him or divorce him because of it. My mother has never had good luck with men, and she wasn't about to blow this. I was just an accessory that came with the marriage."

Emma trailed off, her eyes grave and filled with sorrow.

"When my mother died, Shane fell into a horrible depression. I thought things had been bad before, but now they were even worse. It was like living with a total stranger. Shane wanted nothing to do with me. I'd make his meals and do his laundry, and he'd be polite and thank me… but we were like two strangers in the house. And I tried." Emma's eyes were watering. "I tried everything I could, because he's all I have now. I told you that Shane grew up in foster care and had no family, and my mother was estranged from her parents, so I had no grandparents, and no mother. There was only Shane. And I was so lonely. My mother was my best friend. My only friend. And I wanted to be a family with Shane. More than anything. I just… I wanted someone to love. And I finally had my chance… and your brother took that away from me."

"What do you mean?" Bree asked warily.

Emma crossed her arms. "When I went to the hospital after the car accident, they asked me all kinds of questions. Apparently, it's standard procedure to always ask a woman if there's any chance she's pregnant. When I told them my period was a few days late, they did some blood work, and discovered… they discovered I had been pregnant."

A sick knot rose in Bree's stomach. *Pregnant.* Tyler had gotten Emma pregnant, and then he had taken it away. Emma's stepfather wasn't doing this over bumps and bruises; he was doing it over the death of Emma's child.

"Shane picked me up from the hospital," Emma said, "and the doctor told him everything. There was nothing on his face as he listened to the doctor's words, but I could see the change in his eyes. I know him well enough to know he had died again on the inside… and this time it was because of me. Do you know how awful that feels? To cause pain to someone you care about?"

It was on Bree's tongue to ask *why* Shane would care (since Emma had said Shane had no love for her), but the answer was simple: Shane had lost a grandchild.

Emma looked like she wanted to throw up. "Shane had already suffered so much from my mother's death and their son's death… and then this. How can someone stay sane when all the people you love keep dying? How can anyone handle that?"

"Bad things happen to people," Bree said in a strained voice, "but that's not an excuse to go crazy and do what your stepfather is doing."

"No one can handle that," Emma repeated, as if she didn't hear Bree—or didn't want to hear. "After we got home from the hospital Shane drove off and left. He didn't say where he was going, and I didn't see him again for almost three days. Paul called multiple times looking for him, but I didn't know where he was. He didn't answer the phone for me either. No one had seen him." Emma crossed her arms with a shiver. "And then he came home, and it was like something had… *awoken* inside him. He started asking me questions about Tyler and his family. I was so taken aback that I told him what I knew, which wasn't much. Tyler told me he had two sisters and his parents lived in town, but that was about it. I really didn't stop to think *why* Shane wanted to know, other than he was just trying to make sense of it."

"What happened after that?" Bree asked.

"Shane told me he was going to make things right, and after that everything was going to be different. He didn't say any more than that, and I didn't ask. I was also too afraid to ask what he meant by 'make things right.' Deep down, I knew it wasn't good, and he probably meant to hurt Tyler… but just hurt him. And I'm ashamed to say that there was a small part of me that was okay with that, because Tyler had hurt our family, and that wasn't right. But I never thought he meant to kill Tyler." Emma shook her head. "Two days ago, I was inside the garage getting something from the chest freezer, and I saw the back of his SUV was packed with blankets and food. He didn't say he was going camping or fishing or anything like that, so I didn't know what to think. I didn't want to ask him, because I didn't want him to think I was spying on him. I thought... I was worried he was going to do something bad and then leave town. Abandon me. After he left, I couldn't stop thinking about it, so I used the phone GPS to track him."

"To Alissa," Bree said.

Emma let out a shaky breath. "His phone led me to a back road that led into the camp where you found my SUV. Shane was there, leaving the shelter. He told me again he was going to make things right, and he had Tyler's sister inside the shelter. He didn't tell me anything more than that, only that he needed my help... that we could finish this together."

"You could have gone to the police then," Bree said coldly. "You could have left right then or called them and stopped this."

"I did try to stop him," Emma sputtered. "I begged him not to go through with it, but he wouldn't listen to me. He said he was doing this for our family, and it was the only way to make things right. I should have lied. I should have played along and told him I would help, and then when I was alone, I should have called the police." Her shoulders dropped. "But I didn't do that. I just kept pleading with him. And when he realized I wasn't going to change my mind, he put me in there with Alissa. He locked me in there without a second thought. How could he do that?"

Emma stared vacantly at the floor.

"Listen to me," Bree said, panic filling her chest, "I'm begging you now. You told me you don't want Tyler hurt. Your stepfather's phone isn't working. This Paul guy isn't calling back. We're out of time, and we're out of ideas. Liz was right. We have to call the police and tell them what you know. They can find this factory. They can find it and stop this."

Emma's head moved slowly side to side. "But what if it's not the right place? And I know I can still make things right. If I can get to Shane, and no one is hurt, I can talk some sense into him. I know I can."

"I don't believe that—"

"I don't care what you believe!" Emma fumed. Her eyes locked on to Bree's, and the anger was there again, overtaking Emma's words as her voice rose. "Shane isn't a bad guy! He's not the one who killed my baby!"

Emma's cell phone rang from the corner of the desk, inches from Bree's fingers, and when Bree saw SHANE on the screen, she snatched it without thinking.

"What are you doing?" Emma shouted. "Give that to me!"

"Hello?" Bree answered. Her blood began to boil when there was no response—only breathing—and Bree turned away from Emma, whose face was static with shock.

"This is Bree Walker," Bree said huskily into the phone, "and I want my sister—"

There was a click. Bree's heart crawled into her throat as she pulled the phone from her ear and saw he had ended the call.

"What happened?" Emma asked.

Bree turned away as she swiped to RECENTS and dialed the number. It rang four times, unanswered, and went to voicemail: "Please leave a message."

His voice was low and monotone, and for some reason that pushed a jag of anger through Bree's fear.

"I'll leave a message," she said after the beep. "The message is that I'm at your house, and I know who you are. I know everything. I know what my brother did, and I know why you're doing what you're doing. But hurting Tyler isn't going to bring back Emma's baby. And in case you haven't figured it out yet, you're not the only one here who's angry, and you're not the only one who can hurt people. You may have my brother and sister, but I have your stepdaughter."

Emma's jaw had unhinged as Bree ended the call.

"Don't worry," Bree said, "I already told you earlier I'm not going to hurt you, but if he thinks I'm going to—"

"He doesn't care," Emma choked. "Haven't you been listening to me? He doesn't care about me, and even if he did, he's not going to believe you're going to hurt me." Emma's teeth were clenched and her eyes were two shiny marbles. "Why didn't you let me answer the phone? I was the one he was supposed to talk to. You're only going to make him angry—"

Emma's phone rang, startling them both. Emma tried to grab it from Bree's hand, but Bree was faster and jerked away as she answered.

"Tell me where my sister is," Bree said into the phone.

"We're going to try this again," Shane said, hardening his voice. "I'm going to talk; you're going to listen; and if you have the audacity to try and tell me what to do again, you'll never see your siblings. Do you understand?"

Bree's throat closed. "I—"

"*Do* you understand?"

"Yes," Bree croaked. And just like that, her fear was back, prickling her skin and reminding her that he was in charge—not her—no matter how brave or clever she thought she could be. She almost said more, and it took everything she had to hold her tongue as Shane drew out the silence, as if to test her.

"Good," he finally said. "This doesn't have to be complicated. In fact, I'd prefer it wasn't. We both know your threat about hurting Emma is unfounded, because we both know you won't—not while I have your sister. And I fully expected Emma to tell you everything about me. I sent you there to find her, remember? I told her to tell you nothing, but Emma doesn't exactly have the strongest of wills, and I knew she'd talk. It honestly makes no difference to me what you know at this point. All that matters is Tyler."

"You can't blame him," Bree burst out. "It wasn't his fault Emma crashed and lost the baby. I know you're angry, but this isn't going to get your wife back, and it's not going to make you feel any better. Emma told me what happened with her mother and your unborn son, and I'm so sorry. I'm so sorry for that. And I get that you want revenge on someone, but that someone isn't Tyler. And I know you don't want to do this."

There was only silence from the other end, and a pang of hope rose inside Bree.

"Are you done?" Shane asked. "Have you said your piece? Is it my turn to talk now?"

Bree's mouth went dry. "I just—"

"First of all," he said, his voice briefly climbing to overtake hers, "I apologize for not answering earlier. I slipped outside of cell phone reception range for a short while, and I wasn't able to receive calls. Secondly, Alissa was never meant to be involved, and I'm sorry for that as well. That was partially your fault."

"My fault?"

"I want to be very clear on this point: Emma was *not* involved in what has transpired. She didn't know what I planned to do. What I did, I did of my own free will. Do you understand?"

"Yes," Bree said, looking at Emma, who had given up trying to reclaim her phone and was instead trying to listen. "I understand."

"Good. Now we can move on to your brother. The only thing I knew about Tyler was his first and last name, but that was enough for me to track down your family's trailer in the trailer park. It's not hard to find people in this day and age. Or so I thought. I assumed Tyler lived there, so I waited and watched for days. But there was no Tyler: only you, your mother, and your sister. With each passing day I became more impatient, and then one night, I heard yelling inside the trailer. I could see you and Alissa through the window, shouting at each other."

Bree's stomach churned at the memory.

"Alissa left the trailer and you didn't follow. I waited until Alissa was out of the trailer park before pulling up beside her. When she looked up and made eye contact, I expected to see a furious, hateful expression on her face over what had just occurred... but she wasn't furious. She was crying. This poor girl was in agony over what had just happened."

Don't, Bree tried to say, but her tongue was glued to the top of her mouth.

"I told her I knew Tyler," Shane went on. "Told her that Tyler was in trouble and she was the only one who could help him. She didn't trust me at first; I'll give her that much. But it's not hard to be persuasive. I threw out some generic details about your family, told her I was an old friend of your mother's, and that I could give her a ride to anywhere she wanted to go. I even showed her a photo of my stepdaughter, Emma. If I was a monster who wanted to harm her, why would I carry around a picture of my stepdaughter to show people?"

Bree closed her eyes against her tears.

"And when she still hesitated," Shane said mildly, "I knew I'd have to do things the hard way. That I'd have to forcibly take her and put her into the trunk of my car. No one was around, and while I'm not an intimidating presence, she was a small girl, and in her weakened emotional state of mind—"

"You bastard," Bree said, her voice teetering along a thin, hysterical edge.

"—which is why I was grateful that it didn't come to that," he finished sharply. "Because she opened the door and got inside. I don't think she cared what happened to her at that moment. Didn't care if I was telling the truth or not. She just needed to get away, and I had the ability to take her away. She didn't speak or even look up at me or the road until we were on the highway driving toward the campsite. And by the time she realized I wasn't who I said I was and we had a destination…" Shane let out an exasperated breath. "I'll spare you the details, but your sister wasn't hurt then, and she hasn't been yet. She's merely been detained. And if you do as I say, there's no reason for her to be hurt."

"But not Tyler," Bree said, her voice strained. "You make no promises about him not being hurt, do you?"

"When I end this call," Shane said, "I'm going to send Emma instructions to where I'm at. Tyler is with me. You and Emma come alone. It really is that simple."

"And then what?" Bree asked.

There was a beat of silence. "And then we see what happens next. Are you familiar with the butterfly effect? Each and every choice we make leads us down a different path, and even the most insignificant change can have large effects on the future. If you make the right choices, perhaps things will turn out the way you want."

The fear inside Bree grew. "It doesn't have to be this way. If you tell me you haven't hurt Tyler, I'll believe you. And you said you haven't hurt Alissa, that she's only been detained. There's still time to stop this—"

"It is going to stop… as soon as you and Emma come here."

The called ended. Before Emma could ask, the phone chimed:

Rattay Drive South.

"Where's Rattay Drive?" Bree asked.

"It's the main road we took to get here."

"Where does it go?"

Emma's forehead creased in thought. "It goes for a few miles and eventually leads out of town, but there are lots of side roads that branch off from it."

"And you really think your stepfather is going to be wherever he tells us to go?"

"Yes," Emma said flatly. "My stepfather may be a lot of things, but he doesn't lie or play games. If he says he'll be there, he will."

"And what happens when *we* get there?" Bree asked.

"I don't know, so we better get going. Can I have my phone back now?"

Bree hesitated, realized it didn't matter who had it since they were going together, and passed it to Emma.

"I'm ready," Bree said.

She followed Emma back outside, and Liz immediately emerged from the SUV.

"What's happening?"

"She can't go with us," Emma said to Bree, ignoring Liz.

Liz shot a frantic look at Bree as Emma climbed into the driver's seat. Bree took Liz by the arm and led her to the rear of the SUV.

"It's happening," she told Liz. "We're going to meet him."

Liz paled. "You're going right now? Where?"

"I don't know, but I need you to stay here and call the police."

To Bree's surprise (and relief), Liz didn't argue or protest, only took out her phone. "What do I say?"

"Give them this address. Tell them everything that's happened and tell them to come here." Bree backed away toward the passenger-side door. "You'll be safe when they get here."

"But what about you? Will you be safe?"

Bree hesitated as she opened the passenger side door, tried to think of an answer, and realized she had none to give.

CHAPTER TWENTY-ONE

They drove for what seemed like forever on winding back roads. Emma received new texts every few miles with instructions on which turns to make, leaving Bree to wonder if Shane was tracking them using Emma's phone's GPS. Seeing as how Shane had the knowledge and foresight to disable Alissa's GPS, it wouldn't surprise her. Nothing could surprise Bree at this point. She was fairly certain they were on the outskirts of the neighboring town of Patton City, but even that was nothing more than a calculated guess. Emma had barely breathed since they had left the house, and it was clear from the look on her face (and the weight of her foot on the gas pedal) that she was worried.

"Do you know where he's taking us?" Bree asked, breaking the silence.

"No. I've never been on these roads before."

Emma's phone dinged and Bree caught a glimpse of the screen:

Turn right at the next intersection.

They were definitely being tracked. The feeling was almost as unsettling as being in the middle of nowhere with this girl, not knowing where they were headed, or what was going to happen next.

"It's going to be okay," Emma said, almost too quietly to hear. "Reuman Park."

"Is that where you think we're going?" Bree asked. "To a place called Reuman Park? Is it close?"

Emma glanced over, surprised. It was clear from the expression on her face that she hadn't realized she had spoken the words aloud.

"No," Emma said stiffly. "That's not... It isn't..."

"What?"

Emma fell quiet. Bree was about to press her again when Emma cleared her throat and nodded. "Reuman Park is my happy place," she said, looking at Bree from the corner of her eye. "I know you'll think it's dumb, and I know you don't care about me or my family, but I'm freaking out on the inside, and when I freak out, I get anxious, and I want to throw up. And when that happens, I try to go to my happy place to calm down."

Bree wasn't sure how to respond and remembered Tyler talking about how Emma was a little "off." Her stepfather was a sadistic, cold-hearted abductor, and Emma dealt with it by going to her happy place.

"Shane and my mother had only been dating a few months when he proposed," Emma said, as if Bree was anxiously waiting to hear more. "It wasn't entirely out of the blue. My mother had not so subtly made it clear that she'd marry him if he asked. My mother always wanted to be married, and he was wealthy and provided security. I don't know if she truly loved him, but he seemed to be an honest, decent man, and I think that's all my mother ever wanted. If she didn't love him then, she could learn to love him. And as far as Shane was concerned, he was ... *is*... a man who knows what he wants, and he wanted my mother."

Emma's phone dinged:

Straight for two miles.

"Shane was insistent on a small, no-frills wedding," Emma continued, "and my mother's only request was that it be outside. You only need five people to get legally married in this state: the bride and groom, an officiant, and two witnesses. Paul Varengo was one witness, and his wife was other. They were also the best man and maid of honor." Emma's head tilted, remembering as she spoke. "It was a beautiful day, and after the ceremony, the officiant and Paul and his wife left, and my mother and Shane and I stayed and had a picnic lunch. I had never seen Shane smile so much. He even hugged me. Twice. He had never done that before. Had barely spoken to me before. But as we sat and ate in Reuman Park, everything felt perfect, and for the first time in my life, I felt like I was a part of a family. I felt like I belonged and was loved…"

Bree could feel Emma sneaking glances at her. Bree had nothing to give to this girl. Nothing to say. And because of that, she felt like a monster herself in many ways.

There was another ding from Emma's phone:

Here.

Bree lifted her head, saw nothing outside the window, and was about to speak when she saw light in the distance surrounded by trees, just over the approaching hill.

"Is that what we're looking for?" Bree asked.

Emma leaned forward without answering. Of course it was; there was nothing else around for miles. The SUV's headlights bounced across the dirt road as Emma sped up, and it only took another moment to see it was a small cottage, set off to the right side of the road and lit up like a Christmas tree. Unlike the campsite or the abandoned factory that Emma had speculated about, this place was definitely not deserted. Under different circumstances, the house would have felt picturesque—wooden siding, rock chimney, green shutters—but knowing who was waiting inside chilled Bree's skin.

"Do you know this house?" Bree asked.

"No," Emma said, bringing the SUV to a stop in the empty driveway. "I've never been here before. But I see Shane's car."

Bree followed Emma's finger. A long, brick path lit by short, landscape path lights ran from the back of the house to a large pond lit by an overhead pole light. Shane's car was a few yards away.

"Why did he park all the way out there?" Bree asked.

Emma was already out of the SUV, approaching the house, but she only made it as far as the front step before stopping and looking back. Bree didn't blame her. The last time Emma had encountered her stepfather, he had locked her inside a bomb shelter. And if Shane really was inside, there was no telling what he would do this time. Whatever did happen, Bree was sure of one thing: everything had led to this moment and all the pieces were in place. For better or worse.

"Do we just go inside?" Bree asked, inching forward.

It was a dumb question that didn't need an answer. Emma moved first, opening the screen, but lingered in the threshold. The inside was as rustic as the outside: wooden ceiling beams, a brick fireplace, and leather furniture that looked as if it had never been used. A squat, wooden staircase led to a short hallway with a single closed door on the second floor. Bree's eyes roamed past Emma's shoulder for any signs of her siblings, or signs of struggle, or anything. There was nothing (and no one) in sight, and the only sound was the thump of Bree's pulse inside her temples.

"Hello?" Emma called out, giving Bree a start.

There was no answer. Emma moved to the edge of the living room. Bree followed, trying to see into the tiny kitchen, which was also empty.

"Are you sure you don't know this place?" Bree asked again. "Someone has to live here—"

"They don't."

The voice came from behind them, deep and low. Emma's stepfather was standing at the front door, watching them through the screen. The man in the photograph had been tanned and smiling, but the man across from Bree was a frail carbon copy with heavy bags under his eyes, as if he hadn't slept in days.

A sound left Bree's mouth as Shane came inside, and she instinctively moved backward into the living room, glancing in all directions and realizing the front door was the only way in or out. Shane stood in the entrance, eyes fixed on Bree. He didn't appear anxious or angry, only weary and indifferent.

"No one lives here," Shane said in a hollow voice. "This place was a gift for my wife, Christina. She always said she wanted a small cottage in the woods, and I thought that after our son was born, it would be a tranquil place for her and the baby to spend time together. Lots of fresh air. No noise. But Christina never saw this place. Never even knew about it. It was going to be a surprise, but then my unborn son tried to come into this world and killed her along with himself. This place has sat empty ever since."

Shane raised his hands and shoulders as if to say: *What can you do?* He lowered his head without breaking his stare with Bree. Emma stood motionless by the fireplace as the room lapsed into a thick silence. Bree forced herself not to swallow as she straightened and held his gaze.

"We came," she said to Shane, "just like you told us. I want to see my brother and sister."

"You will," Shane said. "I'm a man of my word." He motioned toward the staircase. "Your brother is upstairs."

Bree's heart quickened as she glanced at the landing above. "What does that mean?"

"It means exactly what it means. Your brother, Tyler, is in the bedroom upstairs. I'm sure he's anxious to see you."

Bree looked up again. The hallway was short, only a few yards in length, with a single closed door at the end.

"This is your one and only chance," Shane said. "And feel free to take your time when you're up there. I need a few words in private with Emma before everything else unfolds."

That was enough to get Bree moving. She shuffled sideways to the staircase and kept her eyes on Shane until she reached the top. She moved toward the doorway on leaden feet, and her hand trembled as she reached for the knob. When she opened the door, there was Tyler, slumped forward in a wooden chair, head bloody, his wrists tied to the wooden armrests.

CHAPTER TWENTY-TWO

"Tyler," Bree gasped, taking three stumbling steps toward him before cupping a hand over her mouth. Tyler's wrists were bound to the chair handles by leather straps—no, leather *belts* that had been cut to a third of their length. There was a gash above his right eyebrow and blood had trickled down one side of his face like a crimson sideburn.

"Open your eyes," Bree said through tears, dropping to her knees. "Come on, Tyler. Wake up."

She worked the buckle holding Tyler's left wrist with trembling fingers, getting nowhere, until—finally—the belt tip slid free of the tongue, sending the left side of Tyler's body forward in the chair. She gave a moan as she clumsily caught him, pushed him back into the chair, and started on the other buckle. This one took less effort, and as soon as his other wrist was free, she shook him by the shoulders and put a shaky hand to his mouth, trying to feel for breath.

"Tyler," she whispered, alternating glances between him and the door, knowing that any second now Emma's stepfather was going to come up and finish the job. Bree pressed a hand to Tyler's chest, trying to find a heartbeat, desperate for any sound, any movement, because it couldn't end like this—

Tyler drew in a gasping breath and rose halfway from the chair.

"It's okay," she said, pushing him back. "I'm here. You're okay."

Tyler lifted his head, his eyes wide and unsettled, taking in the room. "Bree?"

"It's me," she said. "What did he do to you? Did you see Alissa?"

Tyler's hand went to his head, stopping just shy of the gash. "I thought... I thought he was going to kill me."

"Is Alissa here?"

Tyler's face scrunched in pain as he shook his head. "No."

"What do you mean, no? She *has* to be. He told us to come here."

Tyler tried again to get to his feet, and Bree again stopped him. He collapsed back into the chair, breathing heavily.

"Tell me what happened," Bree said. "Tell me everything."

"I called Alissa's phone after I drove away," Tyler said, speaking slowly between shallow breaths. "I kept leaving voicemails and sending texts, telling him I was ready to meet. He eventually texted and told me to start driving south out of town. I did. More texts came, directing me where to go. Eventually the texts led me here."

Tyler closed his eyes. His body was trembling, and Bree didn't know if it was from pain or anger.

"He answered the door when I knocked," Tyler said, "like I was a guest or something. I thought for sure when I saw him I'd know who he was, and why he was doing this, but I've never seen him before—"

"He's Emma's stepfather."

The open-mouthed shock on Tyler's face made it clear that Shane hadn't shared this information.

"Stepfather?" Tyler asked incredulously. "All of this is because of what happened between me and Emma?"

Bree started to answer but realized that if Emma's stepfather hadn't said who he was, there was a good chance Tyler didn't know about the baby.

"Tyler," Bree said, already sick to her stomach, trying to summon the words, "it was more than that. Emma... she was pregnant when she hit the tree when she was leaving Dave's. She lost your baby."

A moment ago, Bree wouldn't have thought Tyler's look of surprise could be surpassed. She was wrong.

"*Baby*?" Tyler croaked.

Bree tried for words, but they only died in her throat. Six hours ago, Bree had arrived home from work, longing for a shower and a hot meal. Now she was inside the house of a maniac, trying to save Alissa's life, telling her brother he was partially responsible for the death of his unborn child…

"You're saying Emma was pregnant with my baby?" Tyler said.

"Yes, and I'm so sorry, but right now we have to—"

"That's impossible. We never had sex."

Now it was Bree's turn to go speechless.

"My baby," Tyler said. "Emma said she was pregnant with *my* baby?"

The question thumped at Bree's brain as she pushed her mind back, replaying the things Emma had said. There had been so much. So many words and emotions. Emma had said she'd gone to the hospital and discovered she was pregnant… but had she actually *said* the baby had been Tyler's? She hadn't. And Bree had never asked her, only assumed it… just as Bree had taken Emma at her word that she had been pregnant and lost a baby. It hadn't occurred to Bree until now that Emma might have been lying about that as well.

"She didn't say you by name," Bree said, trying to reclaim her thoughts, "and I don't even know if she was telling the truth. Right now I don't even care. We have to get you out of here and get Alissa." She looked around the room for anything she might be able to use as a weapon. Outside of a small bed, there was only a nightstand with an alarm clock and a few paperbacks. "How badly are you hurt? Can you walk?"

"I think so," he said, gritting his teeth. "Give me a minute."

Bree grabbed the edge of the bedspread and gingerly wiped the blood from Tyler's forehead and face. The wound itself wasn't as deep as she'd feared, and the bleeding had mostly stopped. Luckily for Tyler, the Walker men had thick skulls—figuratively and literally.

"I wanted to kill him, Bree," Tyler said bluntly. "When he opened that door and I saw him… if there hadn't been a screen door between us, I think I would have gone for his throat. But I didn't, and he told me if I wanted to keep Alissa safe, I needed to do exactly as he said."

Tyler winced, either from pain or remembrance.

"He told me to go upstairs and said he was going to tie me to this chair so I didn't try anything stupid. If I cooperated, he would get Alissa and bring her here. What choice did I have? I knew I could have probably overpowered him, but then what? Beat him bloody until he told me where Alissa was? And what if he didn't tell me? Alissa was already in danger because of me. I couldn't risk it. If this was what I needed to do, then I had to do it."

A noise turned Bree's head, and her pulse quickened as she checked the hallway. It was still empty.

"He tied me up and went to leave," Tyler said, "but when he stopped at the doorway, I knew something was wrong. He stood there for a long time, staring into the floor and taking deep breaths. Then he bent down and picked up something by his feet."

"What?"

"I couldn't tell at first. It was round and gray, and when he turned to face me, I saw it was a concrete pumpkin the size of a baseball. It had been in front of the door as a door stop. When he clutched it in his hand and started toward me, it was pretty obvious what he meant to do."

An icy finger slid down Bree's back.

"I tried to struggle free, but it was no use. The first time he brought it down on my head, my vision doubled. The second time he hit me…" Tyler ran a shaky hand across his mouth. "Everything went black. I don't remember anything else until you showed up just now. I don't even know where he is—"

"He's downstairs," Bree said, shooting a glance over her shoulder. "He told me to come up and get you. I don't know what he's planning to do next."

A grimace crossed Tyler's lips as he fought to get to his feet. Bree quickly hooked her hands under his arm, helping him stand. Tyler touched the back of his head, and even though he hissed in pain, anger settled across his face.

"It doesn't matter what he does," Tyler said. "I'm ready for him this time."

"What do you mean?"

Tyler slipped off his boot and turned it over. The switchblade she had seen at their Uncle Dave's house dropped into his hand. "I hid it in my boot before I came here, just in case."

"What are you going to do?" Bree asked.

"If he doesn't give us our sister," Tyler said in a voice that wasn't quite steady, "I'm going to kill him."

CHAPTER TWENTY-THREE

"Are you ready?" Tyler asked.

Bree gave a terrified nod. She wasn't, but there was no other option. However this played out, it was going to happen right here, right now. She knew that much.

Bree stayed behind Tyler as he made his way slowly toward the door, wobbling with each step, with one hand in front to steady himself. When he took a pained breath and almost lost his balance, Bree grabbed his arm.

"Give me the knife," Bree said.

Tyler righted himself as he shook his head. "No."

"You can barely stand," she said, lowering her voice. They were just shy of the door and she gripped his arm more tightly. "We need to think this through."

"There's nothing to think through—"

"Nothing about this makes sense. Emma's stepfather was so desperate to get you that he abducted Alissa. He *abducted* her in order to get to you. But when you came here, the only thing he did was tie you to a chair and get angry enough to hit you a few times. He told Emma to bring me here, and he sent me up here, knowing full well I would set you free. He did it without a second thought. Why would he do that? Nothing about this feels right."

"It doesn't have to feel right," Tyler said. "Nothing about this makes sense. For all we know, he realized how messed up this is or had a change of heart."

Bree's stomach turned to lead. "Or maybe the reason he wants everyone in one place is because he's planning to kill us all. Did you think of that? No witnesses and no one left alive."

"That's not going to happen," Tyler said, pulling free from Bree's grip. "I'm not going to let anything happen to you or Alissa. I don't know what he's planning to do, but I'm ready for anything he tries. Get behind me and stay behind me."

Tyler stepped across the bedroom threshold into the hallway. Bree followed. The voices downstairs had stopped, and when Bree looked over the railing, there was only Shane standing by the fireplace, looking back up at them. Tyler held the knife behind his back, inches from where Bree was clutching onto the back of his shirt.

"I see you found your brother," Shane called up.

"Where's Emma?" Bree asked.

"Emma is no longer your concern," Shane said evenly.

"What does that mean?"

"I don't care about Emma," Tyler said, "or you, or why you're doing this. I only care about Alissa. I did as you asked. You wanted me here; I'm here. I let you tie me to a chair—"

"Only to keep you restrained while I finished doing what needed to be done." Shane shook his head as if shedding unwanted thoughts. "I shouldn't have hit you when you were incapacitated. I momentarily lost control. I apologize."

"I don't want your apology," Tyler said tightly, "I want Alissa. You either tell me where my sister is, or I'm going to come down there and make you tell me."

Tyler took two steps forward using the rail for support and balance, trying not to reveal how weak he really was. He wasn't succeeding. Bree knew the look on Tyler's face: he was in fight or flight mode, but there was no option for flight, and he was in no condition to fight.

"Do you remember our conversation earlier?" Shane asked, and Bree realized he was speaking to her. "About the butterfly effect?

How even one tiny change of events can cause massive disruption to so many lives—"

"We're not doing this," Tyler said, his voice edged with contempt. "I don't care what twisted and deranged thought-process brought you to this point; I just want our sister."

Shane looked momentarily bemused. "And I'm trying to accomplish that by explaining. But you don't understand that, do you? You're just a blunt object without compassion or understanding. Fine. Time's short anyway. You want to get to it, let's get to it."

Bree stiffened as Shane approached the staircase. There was nothing visible in his hands, but that didn't mean he didn't have something hidden, like Tyler.

"You killed Emma's child," Shane said, the words trembling on his lips.

"Emma got into a car accident," Tyler said. "She hit a tree and lost the baby. I wasn't driving—"

"But it was because of you. Maybe you didn't cause it directly or purposely, but you are responsible. I hold you responsible."

"But that's crazy," Bree said. "Emma shouldn't have been driving if she was that upset, and her causing her own accident doesn't make Tyler a murderer. You can't honestly believe Tyler's to blame. You can't. It's not right. You have to see that…"

Bree hand's continued through the air as she ran out of words, waiting for Shane to angrily interrupt. To talk over her. Argue and tell her otherwise. But Shane only watched and waited, as if he were a man with no cares in the world.

"I'm not going to ask you again," Tyler said.

"No? Then I had better make my retort fast. Your sister Bree told me earlier that I was doing this out of revenge for Christina, my wife. That I wanted revenge on the world because she died along with my child, and in a way, she was right. All this world has done is take from me. I never knew my real parents. If I have siblings, I don't know them and never will. I never knew love until I met Christina. She was all I had. She was my family."

"You have Emma," Bree said. "She's your family. She loves you."

Shane's lips thinned. "But she's not mine. Maybe that's horrible to say, but she was fourteen when I came into her life. She wasn't a child to be raised; she was already a young woman. She knew how to take care of herself. The only thing I had to offer her was my money... which she happily took."

Shane wasn't looking at them but through them, his eyes distant and glassy.

"This world has taken so much from me," Shane said, "and I believed I finally had a chance to take something from the world. One last chance for me to right all the wrongs... but even that was taken away. Emma's child was my chance. And now I again have nothing."

"What do you mean *your* chance?" Bree asked carefully.

Shane's mouth quivered. "The baby was mine."

A sound came from deep in Tyler's throat, but no words left his mouth.

"Emma's baby," Shane said, speaking the words quietly, as if wrestling with the enormity of it, "was mine. My child. I'm not going to try to make you understand—"

"You're sick," Tyler said. His face and arms had drained of color. "How could you do that to her? She's a child to you. Your *daughter*."

"Stepdaughter," Shane said. His head was lowered, his face unreadable. "I'm not a monster. I'm just a man who was trying to make things right. To create some balance in the universe."

"Taking revenge on Tyler won't solve anything," Bree said with a frustrated cry. "No matter what Tyler did or didn't do, hurting our family isn't going to bring back your wife or child, and you're a pathetic coward if you think otherwise."

"A true coward would have given up," Shane said. "A true coward would have hung himself from the center beam in the attic of his house using the yellow, nylon rope he had recently purchased at the local hardware store. Or he might have taken the revolver from the gun safe in his basement, placed it into his mouth, and pulled the trigger."

"Then do it," Tyler said tersely. "If you want to kill yourself, then kill yourself."

Bree gasped. "Tyler—"

"Stay out of this," Tyler hissed at Bree, moving to the top of the staircase. "I still don't know what the hell you want, but I'm done listening to you talk. You tell me where our sister is, or I'm going to come down there and make you tell me."

Fear sunk into Bree's bones as she waited for Shane to speak. Tyler had reached his breaking point and she knew it.

"Suicide is the coward's way out," Shane said, "and if I took my own life, there would be no justice for Emma's child. There has to be justice. A life for a life."

Tyler's lips moved, but it was Bree who spoke: "What does that mean?"

"This was never about killing Tyler," Shane said. "The dead don't suffer. It's the ones who are left *behind* who suffer." His eyes narrowed on Tyler. "What would make you suffer, Tyler? What are your weaknesses? Is it your girlfriends? Your mother? Maybe your sister, Alissa? Would the loss of *both* your sisters make you suffer? The loss of both of my unborn children has made me suffer."

"Last chance," Tyler said.

"Alissa had weaknesses," Shane said. "We talked about them when she was my guest. She was hesitant at first, but eventually with some cajoling, she told me. We share a fear of spiders, her and me. She's also scared of heights, but I'm not. I'm also not terrified of water, like she is." Shane lifted his head. "Did you know about her fear of water? Alissa can't swim. Not at all. Not even one… tiny… bit."

Terror froze Bree's muscles. "The pond," she croaked at Tyler. "When Emma and I got here we saw Shane's car around back next to a pond—"

"Does Bree have any weaknesses, I wonder?" Shane asked. For the first time, there was anger behind Shane's eyes and malice in his voice. "I bet she has a weakness for pain. Let's find out. I'm feeling generous, Tyler, so this time, you get to *watch*."

Shane reached around to his back pocket as if going for a weapon, and everything that happened next happened fast.

Tyler let out a bellow of rage. He catapulted himself down the staircase, hit Shane squarely in the chest, and sent them both reeling across the floor in a tumbling mass of elbows and knees.

"Don't!" Bree shouted at Tyler.

It was too late. The knife in Tyler's hand did its work—slicing and cutting and digging into Shane's chest. Blood spurted. Shane screamed. Bree screamed.

And as quickly as it began, it was over.

Tyler rolled away from Shane, his breath coming in short clips of air. The bloody knife fell from Tyler's fingers as Bree gripped the railing with both hands to keep from collapsing.

"Don't," Bree said again, barely voicing the word.

Shane lay on his back, staring into the ceiling, gurgling blood. His left hand rose a few inches off the floor before dropping back into the carpet, fingers twitching.

"*What did you do?*"

Bree craned her head toward the voice below. Emma was just inside the doorway with both hands clamped over her mouth, but she wasn't alone. Through Bree's fog of tears, she could make out another shape standing behind Emma, but it wasn't until Emma moved forward that Bree saw the girl's face.

"Alissa?" Bree rasped.

Bree was down the stairs in the blink of an eye, pushing past Emma and clutching onto Alissa hard enough to squeeze the air from her lungs.

"You're alive," Bree said, pulling away momentarily to make sure it really was Alissa before embracing her again. "I thought… he said—"

"Why?" Emma cried. She was kneeling beside Shane, gripping his hand tightly in hers. Her eyes moved between Tyler and Bree, her cheeks streaming with tears. "I was getting Alissa. When you went upstairs, Shane told me Alissa was locked inside the trunk of his car, and I was supposed to let her out and bring her inside, and that's what I was doing. I was getting her!"

Bree tightened her grip on Alissa as Tyler worked himself to his feet like a man drugged. His head turned sluggishly, first to Shane, then Emma, and finally Alissa.

"You're alive," he said breathlessly. His lips moved as if he wanted to say more, but he only looked down at the back of his hand, which was lined with streaks of blood.

"Help me," Emma moaned, digging her phone from her pocket. "We need to call for help—"

"Emma…" Shane was trying to speak. His eyes were closed, but he was trying and failing to lift his head. Emma cradled the back of his neck and leaned over him close enough to put her ear next to his mouth.

Alissa began to tremble violently as she stared at Shane with wide eyes.

"Don't look at him," Bree said, trying to turn Alissa's head as she herself continued to gape, unable to look away. "He can't hurt you now."

"He didn't," Alissa said. "He told me if I cooperated with him, no one would get hurt, so I *did*." Alissa's voice, already wavering, now broke. "I asked myself what you would have done, and I know you would have fought and tried to escape, but I'm not as brave as you, and I was scared, and I'm so sorry, Bree—I should have listened to you, and I shouldn't have gotten mad that night and left—" Alissa burst into tears.

"This isn't your fault," Bree said, firming her voice as Alissa's cries intensified. "You didn't cause this."

No one did, Bree wanted to say… but as she stared into Tyler's dazed face, she couldn't say it. And maybe that wasn't fair, but right now, at this moment, she didn't care.

Shane's chest had stopping rising and falling. Emma was crying and trying to dial her phone.

Tyler took a hesitant step toward her. "Emma," he said, his voice hoarse and brittle. "I'm… I didn't…"

"Go away," Emma sobbed. The phone rose and fell from her ear as if she didn't have the strength to hold it. "I have to call for help."

"Nine-one-one," a female voice answered loudly enough that Bree could hear it from where she stood. "What's your emergency?"

A small click escaped Emma's throat, but nothing more. The phone dipped in Emma's hand, and Bree moved forward without thinking and took it from her.

"What's your emergency?" the dispatcher asked again.

"There's been an accident," Bree said into the phone. "We need an ambulance, but I don't know exactly where we are."

"We can trace the call," the dispatcher replied. "Can you give me the nature of the accident?"

Bree looked at Shane, then over at Emma, who was still crying with her face now buried in her hands.

"Ma'am?" the dispatcher asked again. "Can you give me the nature of the accident?"

"It's just that," Bree said quietly. "An accident. Please hurry."

She set Emma's phone on the table as the dispatcher continued to ask questions, but Bree had no more answers to give.

CHAPTER TWENTY-FOUR

Bree Walker was tired.

It had already been a long day at the grocery, and as much as she wanted to go home and get off her feet, family came first. It had been almost a week since that night at Shane's cottage, and in that time, they had only been allowed to see Tyler once. Most of their time had been spent speaking with the attorney, who Bree still had no idea how they were going to pay.

"But it could always be worse," Bree said under her breath as she wheeled her truck into the police station parking lot... although this time, she wasn't sure if she truly believed that. As if to test that theory, Bree's heart ground to a halt as she saw Emma exiting the police station accompanied by a tall man dressed in a dark suit and carrying a briefcase. This was the last thing Bree wanted to deal with right now, and she tried to duck to one side as she parked, but it was no use—Emma had spotted her, said something to the man, and was headed Bree's way. Bree took a steadying breath as she cut the engine.

"Bree," Emma said, leaning into the driver-side window. "I've been trying to get ahold of you. Did you get my message?"

Message was an understatement; Emma had sent multiple texts over the latter half of the week, sometimes twice a day. Tyler's attorney had advised everyone in Bree's family against speaking to Emma, and from the look on Emma's attorney's face, she was being told the same.

"What do you want, Emma?" Bree asked.

Emma gave Bree a confused, almost offended frown, sending a tick of disquiet through Bree. Emotional bonds were often created when individuals went through stressful and dangerous situations together, and Emma clearly felt that she and Bree now had some intimate connection. But Bree didn't feel that way. Not by a long shot. As far as Bree was concerned, Emma had been the catalyst for all of this, and Bree wanted nothing to do with her. If Emma hadn't followed Tyler, she wouldn't have crashed her SUV. And if she hadn't crashed the SUV, she wouldn't have lost the baby. And if she hadn't told Shane what had happened, Shane wouldn't have sought revenge on Tyler.

But there was another part of Bree that knew better. A part of her that had already lost countless hours of sleep replaying the sequence of events in her head, assigning and shifting blame not only to Emma and Shane and Tyler, but also to herself for causing the argument that drove Alissa out of the trailer that night. No, there was plenty of blame to be passed around for all of them.

"Ms. Lockhart," the man spoke up, "it's not in your best interest to speak directly with Ms. Walker. I'd advise—"

"I don't care what you advise," Emma said without breaking eye contact with Bree. "I'm advising you give us a moment or I'll find a different law firm to hire with my stepfather's money."

The man's expression didn't change, but he seemed to know better than to argue. Attorneys were plentiful in this town (Bree's mother had called almost a dozen before settling on the law firm of Randon, Cline, and Green), and there was easily a small fortune to be made due to the complexities of this case. Tyler had committed murder, but Shane had abducted their sister, and one could argue that Tyler had acted in self-defense.

Emma was still watching Bree with doe eyes, and it became painfully clear that she had no intention of leaving. When Bree exited the truck, Emma tried to take Bree by the hand, as if to lead her away.

"Don't touch me," Bree said roughly. "I'm not interested in going anywhere with you, and everyone says we shouldn't talk, so let's just leave it at that."

"I want to explain some things to you."

"There's nothing to explain," Bree said, starting for the entrance. "I have nothing to say—"

"My stepfather was dying of bone cancer."

"Ms. Lockhart," the man said sharply, trying to position himself between them, as if that somehow might deflect what was being said. "You can't discuss—"

This time when Emma took Bree by the hand, Bree was too stunned to resist. She led Bree away from her truck and gave her attorney the death glare.

"*Don't* follow us," Emma seethed, "or you're fired. I mean that."

Bree shook her hand free as she looked at Emma's attorney, who had abandoned trying to intercede and pulled out his cell phone, undoubtedly to call someone at the main office. Emma had gall; Bree would give her that much.

"I know you don't want to talk to me," Emma said, "but I have to tell you some things, and you have to listen. I can make things go easier for Tyler when they ask me questions, but not if you keep fighting against me. I want to be in Tyler's corner, because I want to help. That's all I've tried to do this whole time: help. I didn't want any of this to happen, and I tried to stop it. I'm not my stepfather. Shane did this to your family—not me."

A spark of anger flickered inside Bree at Emma's continued insistence at minimizing the part she played in this, but Bree knew Emma was right about one thing: she could help Tyler. Emma had direct insight into Shane, and because of that, Emma's testimony would carry a lot of weight. Having Shane's stepdaughter on Tyler's side would go a long way in Tyler's favor. If that meant Bree had to listen to whatever nonsense Emma felt the need to spew, Bree could listen for one last time.

"Okay," she told Emma, unable to keep a tremor from her voice. "So talk."

Emma's attorney was still on his phone, speaking rapidly and quietly, and Emma stepped out of sight behind a parked van.

"Payment has to be made," Emma said to Bree.

Bree's mouth went dry. "What?"

"That was the last thing Shane said to me before he died. Payment has to be made."

"I don't understand—"

"Everyone who knew Shane knew one thing about him: he believed in justice and balance above all else. If he wronged someone, he would do whatever it took to make things right. But at the same, if someone wronged him, they were his enemy… unless they made amends on their own."

"So what happened to Tyler is his own fault because he didn't make 'amends' with your stepfather over something he didn't even know he did? Is that what you're trying to *explain*? Because if so, that's bullshit, and I'm not going to stand here while you defend your stepfather."

"I'm not *defending* him," Emma said with a jag of anger in her voice. "I'm trying to make you understand why Shane did what he did. Shane knew what he was doing to your family was wrong, but he still went ahead with it because he knew what Tyler would do in return. In Shane's mind, this was the only way there could be justice for everyone."

Bree gave a disgusted grunt. "You're as crazy as he was. Are you even listening to yourself? Where's the justice in Tyler going to prison because he wronged your family?"

"Tyler's going to prison for killing my stepfather."

"Because Shane gave him no choice—"

"*Bad things happen to people*," Emma said in a mechanical voice, "*but that's not an excuse to go crazy*. Your words. It's what you said to me at my house earlier. But isn't that exactly what Tyler did:

go crazy and kill my stepfather because something bad happened? Explain to me how that makes him different from Shane, because if Tyler hadn't made the choice he did, then Shane would still be alive, and Tyler wouldn't be sitting in jail right now."

Bree opened her mouth and closed it. She realized she had no answer, because Emma was right.

Emma's chest deflated. "I'm not defending Shane. What he did was wrong. I just want you to understand that he wasn't *evil*. He had lost all hope and was sick."

"We agree on that much," Bree said, finding her voice. "Anyone who would do what he did to you is *beyond* sick."

"I'm not Shane's biological daughter," Emma said, bristling, "and I'm eighteen—"

"And you keep saying you're not defending him, yet here you are, defending him again. He was your stepfather and he…" Bree couldn't bring herself to say it.

"Impregnated me?" Emma asked. "Knocked me up? Did you ever stop to think that maybe that wasn't his idea? Maybe it was mine."

"Yours?"

"When I found out Shane had cancer a few months ago, I was devastated. He was all I had in this world, and I had hoped that over time we could be a family. All we had was each other, and I had hoped he'd see that." Emma drew a shallow breath. "If Shane died, I would have no one at all. Can you understand that? No parents or siblings or aunts or uncles or grandparents or any extended family… there would be *no* one. I would be alone on this planet."

Emma fell quiet as a girl walked past and gave them a smile. Bree halfheartedly returned it and waited for Emma to continue.

"I went to visit my mother," Emma said. "I go to her grave a few times a week, and I sit there and talk to her and sometimes ask her questions. I asked her what I should do… and she told me. Her voice came back to me, clear as day, and said I needed a child. A child would give Shane a way for him to live on when he died, and it would also give me someone to love. Shane was against the idea when I first asked, but I knew he was lonely, and since I look like my mother—"

"Stop," Bree said as her stomach turned itself inside out. "I don't want to hear anymore. I have to go inside. I need to see Tyler."

"I have something for you," Emma said, digging into her purse and pulling out a tan envelope. "I was going to have someone drop this by your trailer. I've been carrying it for the last two days."

"What is it?" Bree asked warily.

"The only way I know how to help your family and make amends for mine. And you're going to hate me for it."

Bree took it. Emma turned without another word and brushed past her attorney, whose eyes were fixed on the envelope in Bree's hand. For a moment, Bree thought he was going to ask for it—maybe even try to *demand* it—but he only pursed his lips and trailed after Emma. Bree broke the envelope's seal, already knowing what was inside, because there was only one thing it could be.

The check was made out to Bree Walker. It was for $10,000.

Bree stared at it without blinking. Her hand didn't tremble. Her heart didn't race. She only felt empty. This amount of money was probably nothing to Emma, but it would change everything for Bree and her family… even if it was blood money.

Payment has to be made.

Bree returned the check to the envelope and carefully placed it into her back pocket. For now, it would have to be enough.

For now.

CHAPTER TWENTY-FIVE

It was almost ten o'clock when Bree and her mother arrived at Kistner's, a small restaurant in the downtown area, nestled between a frozen yogurt shop and a clothing store. There was a neon OPEN sign in the front window, but only a few people were inside, and all the metal chairs out front had been stacked and moved off to one side.

"We don't have to do this," Bree said to her mother again. "We have enough on our plate right now as it is."

"I know," Cassie said earnestly, "but he said it was important. And you didn't have to come—"

"The last time he set foot inside our trailer you ended up with a fractured wrist. There's no way I'm letting you meet him alone, even if it is in a public place."

"I think I'll be okay."

"I know you will," Bree said, pulling open the heavy doors, "because I'll be right beside you to make sure of it. You're not sending me away this time."

The inside of the restaurant was dark and cool. Soft music wafted down from overheard, mostly acoustic guitar, and aromas out of their price range lingered in the air. The long, mahogany counter that ran the length of the inside wall had been wiped clean, and almost all the tables had been reset with fresh tablecloths, glasses, and silverware rolled in napkins.

The kitchen door banged open, turning both their heads. The waitress was college-aged with heavy eyeliner and made no attempt to mask her displeasure at the sight of them. Bree knew the look well: it was the "last-minute customer" face. Bree knew she was guilty of making that face herself on more than one occasion at the grocery store.

"I'm sorry," the waitress said, not sounding sorry at all, "but the kitchen has already started to close, so if you're trying to eat—"

"We're not," Cassie said. "We're supposed to meet someone here, but I don't think he's arrived."

The waitress raised her eyebrows as if to say *and?* but that was all Bree's mother had to offer.

"We'll only need a few minutes," Bree added, mostly to say something. "I promise it will be a quick conversation, and then we'll go. We'll probably even be gone before those other people are."

Bree motioned at the middle-aged man and woman seated at the corner table talking quietly amongst themselves. The girl shot an impatient look at the clock, started to speak, seemed to think better of it, and manufactured an exaggerated smile.

"Let me know if you need anything," the girl said, and promptly walked away before giving either of them a chance to answer.

"I'd better pee," Cassie told Bree. "I need a clear head *and* bladder for this conversation."

She made for the restrooms. Bree took a seat at the closest table and tried not to disturb the place settings. Her throat felt like sandpaper and some water would have been nice, but she told herself she could survive without it. It wasn't so much that she thought the girl would spit in it, although that was a definite possibility; it was more that the waitress probably still had fifty million things to do before her night ended, and even little things—like fetching water—would slow her down. If Bree's mother had taught her anything, it was that waitressing was a tough, demanding job that didn't always pay all the bills.

Bree started to look over her shoulder toward the restrooms when she caught sight of him through the front window, looking in. He opened the door and stepped inside but only went as far as the threshold. The waitress was there in a flash, blocking his path and shaking her head.

"Kitchen's closed," she told him. "We reopen tomorrow at eleven."

Bree couldn't hear his mumbled response, but she heard the waitress sigh, turn, and shoot a look at Bree before locking the door behind him. Her eyes found Bree again as she passed by the table and said, "Five minutes."

"Sure," Bree muttered as her father approached, looking as confused and uncomfortable as Bree did.

"Your mother was supposed to come," he said, stopping shy of the table.

"She's using the bathroom. She'll be out in a minute."

It was clear from the expression on his face that he wasn't entirely convinced this was the truth, but he took the seat across from her. It had only been a week since she had gone to his apartment looking for Tyler, but in that short time, he looked like he had lost weight. His face wasn't as full as she remembered, and his skin seemed pale and washed out, even under the dim lighting.

"Your mother's taking her sweet time as always," Jack said, even though he had only been seated for a few seconds. He made a guttural sound as he searched for the waitress. "I need a drink—"

"Why don't you just tell me what you have to say and then go," Bree said pointedly. "I'll be sure to pass it along."

Jack sized Bree up with a shake of his head. "Remind me again at what point you decided to appoint yourself the matriarch of our family, because the last time that I checked—"

He straightened as Cassie appeared. She sat next to Bree, her face set in stone. Jack leaned back in the chair but left his hands on the table. It was difficult to be sure, but it looked like his hands were shaking, if only a little. His eyes skipped from Cassie to Bree.

"Can we have a moment alone?" he asked Bree.

"Anything you have to say to me," Cassie said, "you can also say in front of our daughter."

There was a flicker of something in his eyes—not anger... more surprise, because this was not the way her mother talked to her father. At least, it hadn't been in all their years of marriage. To Bree's knowledge, in the six months since he had left, her mother and father had only corresponded a handful of times—always over the phone, and only for a few moments.

"Fine," he said. He drew a breath through his nose and lowered his chin. "When I learned what happened to Alissa, it shook me to the core. Bree never told me why she was looking for Tyler that night, and if she had..." He raised his hands, as if the words didn't have to be said, before leveling his stare at Bree. "I wish you would have told me, but I know you had no reason to trust that I'd do the right thing. I've never given you a reason to trust me. I've never given anyone in this family a reason to trust me. That's on me."

He paused, giving Bree or Cassie a chance to respond, and cleared his throat and continued when they didn't.

"I don't feel the need to rehash what happened six months ago, but I made a horrible mistake that night. I've made many mistakes in my life and in our marriage. I should *thank* Bree for stopping me that night before I seriously injured anyone."

Jack's piercing gaze was anything but thankful, and Bree took her mother's hand under the table.

"What I'm trying to say is that I'm not the same person I was six months ago. I know it's easy to sit here and say that, but it's true. I'm not even the same person I was a week ago. I've done a lot of soul-searching, and I want to make some changes. I've thought a lot about this, and I think we should do a paternity test."

Cassie's expression didn't change, but Bree could feel her mother's hand trembling in trepidation, anger, or both. A few weeks after that night at the trailer, Bree had caught Alissa looking at paternity test kits on her laptop. Bree had done her own research after that and discovered that the home versions were common and surprisingly inexpensive, but they often produced mixed results. Bree wasn't even sure how something like that would work, seeing as how the two men in question were brothers. Regardless, it had never come up once with Alissa or their mother. Until now.

"And what would you do with the results of a paternity test?" Cassie asked.

The question seemed to catch him off guard. "What do you mean?"

"If the test proved Alissa *wasn't* yours, what would you do?"

Jack firmed his jaw. This wasn't a question he expected.

"Or let's say the test *did* prove Alissa was yours," she continued. "What then? Would you finally speak to her again? Resume the role of playing her father from a distance? Or is this information just for your own knowledge, so you can save face every time you look in the mirror, knowing you didn't spend the last sixteen years raising your brother's daughter as your own?"

Jack's knuckles tightened on the table. Bree had never once seen her mother push her father like this, but a lot had changed in the last six months, including the introduction of a restraining order. Bree had been beyond surprised when her mother had agreed to meet Jack when he asked—the distance across a restaurant table was clearly less than a hundred yards—but now Bree realized maybe this had been her mother's plan all along: to finally, for the first time in her life, have the freedom to say what she wanted to say and release years of pent-up anger and frustration.

"When I came back from the bathroom," she went on, "it sounded like you were lecturing Bree on the roles we play in this family. I hope not, because you of all people should know how much Bree has sacrificed. Not only has she helped raise Tyler and Alissa, she started working at age sixteen to help pay the bills. She could have gone away to college after high school—she was smart enough and could have easily gotten financial aid—but she didn't. She also could have moved out of the trailer and gotten an apartment with friends, but instead she chose to stay with us." Her voice cracked as she continued. "And some days that breaks my heart, because I *do* want Bree to have her own life... but I also know that someday she will, and this world is going to repay her a thousand times over for all she's done. And when that day comes and she does leave, I'll know I can still count on Bree to be there for us. And do you know why?"

Jack only stared at her, and Cassie drew out the silence, waiting for at minimum an acknowledgment, if not an answer.

"Why?" Jack asked flatly.

"Because a real family sticks together... no matter what. Not because they feel they have to, and not because blood is thicker than water, and not because of what some test says. They stick together because they know they can't make it in this world without each other. *That's* what it means to be a family."

Cassie leaned forward, almost close enough to reach out and touch him.

"I'll talk to Alissa about a paternity test, but ultimately, the decision will be hers to make. I won't begrudge her the right to know the truth. But if she agrees to the test, I'm telling you this right now, Jack: no matter what the results say, Alissa isn't yours or Dave's—she's *mine*. She always has been, and she always will be."

She pushed away from the table and stood.

"I'm ready to go, Bree. My head hurts, and I think everyone here has said what they came to say."

Bree rose to her feet as Cassie started for the door. Maybe her mother had nothing more to say, but Bree did, and she lingered at the table until he looked at her.

"I saw a bumper sticker on a truck the other day," she told him. "It said, 'Holding onto anger is like swallowing poison and expecting the other person to die.' Maybe it sounds dumb to say that I took a bumper sticker to heart, but after everything that happened, that's what I did. And that made me do some soul-searching myself. I don't hate you. Not anymore. I know family is messy and people do the wrong things for the right reasons and vice versa, but after what happened with Emma and her stepfather… after seeing how hate and anger can drive people to do horrible things and hurt others…"

Bree tried to find the remaining words. Tried to convey everything she was feeling, knowing she couldn't. Knowing there was no way to make him understand, that she didn't fully understand.

"I don't hate you," Bree said again, "and someday I hope to begin the process of forgiving you. But even if that happens, I will never forget the things you've done. If you really want to try and make things right with this family, go see Tyler. He needs you. You said you wished I'd asked for help with Alissa; now I'm asking for help with Tyler. If you can do that, then maybe I can learn to forgive… Dad."

Bree joined her mother at the doorway and cast a glance back at her father. He was still at the table, hunched forward, staring into nothingness.

"Do people ever change?" Bree asked her mother.

"Yes," Cassie replied without hesitation. "If they truly want to, they do."

"Will he?"

Her mother didn't answer. She only took Bree's hand, squeezed, and led Bree out of the door.

A LETTER FROM ERIK

I want to say a huge thank you for choosing to read *I Know You*. If you did enjoy it, and want to keep up-to-date with all my latest releases, just sign up at the following link. Your e-mail address will never be shared and you can unsubscribe at any time.

www.bookouture.com/erik-therme

When I started writing *I Know You*, I had no idea who had abducted Alissa or for what reason—I only knew it was up to Bree to get her back. It wasn't until I finished the first draft that I realized the story wasn't about a missing girl; it was about family. I was blessed to grow up in a stable, loving environment, but not all of my childhood friends had that luxury, and it's definitely had a lasting impact on their lives—good and bad. Bree has a complicated relationship with her mother and siblings, but there's also love and loyalty, if not always respect and patience. I don't know what the future holds for the Walkers, but whatever it is, I know they'll face it together.

I hope you loved *I Know You*, and if you did, I would be very grateful if you could write a review. I'd love to hear what you think, and it makes such a difference helping new readers to discover one of my books for the first time.

I love hearing from my readers—you can get in touch on my *Facebook* page, through *Twitter*, *Goodreads* or my *website*.

Thanks,
Erik Therme

ErikTherme.writer

ErikTherme

7831573.erik_therme

www.bookbub.com/authors/erik-therme

ACKNOWLEDGEMENTS

First and foremost, thanks to Josh Stilley (as always) for answering my steady stream of ridiculous medical questions. It's not uncommon for Josh to open an e-mail and see something along the lines of: "So, hypothetically… what are some diseases that might have been prevalent in the 1980s that would affect a person's central nervous system—including their pinky fingers and big toes—and how might that limit their ability to climb walls using a grappling hook?" I exaggerate, of course, but not by much.

My second round of thanks goes to my editor, Lydia Vassar-Smith, for her endless patience through the multiple (and sometimes brutal) merry-go-round of structural edits. Lydia and I don't always see eye to eye, but she's fair and challenging with her edits, and as much as it pains me to admit it, she's usually right.

Last, but certainly not least, a tremendous amount of thanks to the marketing "heart and soul" of Bookouture: Noelle Holten and Kim Nash. These two work tirelessly at promoting Bookouture's books, and I think I speak for all us authors when I say we are beyond blessed to have them.

CPSIA information can be obtained
at www.ICGtesting.com
Printed in the USA
FFHW021825020419
51457686-56907FF